"I should get moving, too," Jake said with some hesitance. "Will you be okay? Do you want to call someone to stay with you?"

"I'll be fine," Rachel replied. "I'm a lot tougher than I look."

A faint smile tipped his lips. "So I've noticed. You paint, you plow snow, you run a successful business, and you even make a decent cup of coffee. I'm impressed."

"Don't be," she said, smiling. "It's all smoke and mirrors."

"No, it isn't," he returned. "It's all you." Then out of the blue, the night seemed to shrink around them, his gaze softened when he looked at her. "You're an extraordinary woman, Rachel."

Books by Lauren Nichols

Love Inspired Suspense

Marked for Murder
On Deadly Ground

LAUREN NICHOLS

From the time Waldenbooks bestselling author Lauren Nichols was able to read, there was a book in her hand—then later, in her mind. Happily, her first attempt at romantic fiction was a finalist in RWA's Golden Heart Contest, and though she didn't win, she's been blessed to sell eight romantic suspense novels, and dozens of romance, mystery and science-fiction short stories to national magazines. This is her second Christian romantic suspense novel for Love Inspired Books.

When Lauren isn't working on a project or hanging out with her family and friends, she enjoys gardening, geocaching and traveling anywhere with her very best friend, her husband, Mike. Lauren loves to hear from readers. You can email her at lauren_nich@yahoo.com or through her website, www.laurennicholsbooks.yolasite.com.

On DEADLY GROUND

Lauren Nichols

Love Inspired

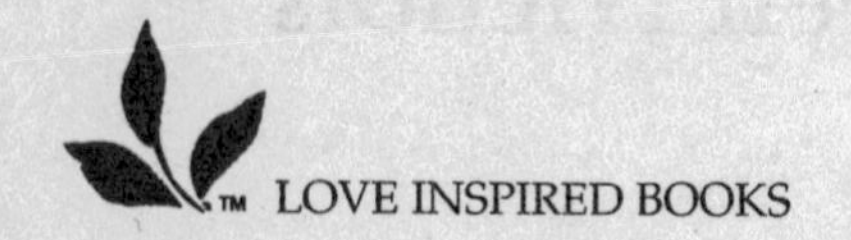

Recycling programs for this product may not exist in your area.

ISBN-13: 978-0-373-44455-7

ON DEADLY GROUND

This edition published by arrangement with Love Inspired Books,

www.LoveInspiredBooks.com

Printed in U.S.A.

The Lord is close to the brokenhearted; He rescues those who are crushed in spirit.

—*Psalms* 34:18

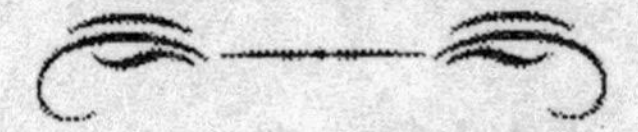

For Good Friends Old and New.

For the gang from Fisher's Big Wheel,
and for Allison, Louise and
Ken "Tiki" Soeder. You guys make me smile.

And always for Mike.

Acknowledgments

My thanks to Richard Peck,
who taught me how to sabotage a bulldozer.

No worries, my friend. I'll leave yours alone!

ONE

Sighing, Rachel Patterson squinted at the clock on her nightstand, saw that it was only 2:00 a.m., then groaned, flipped over and burrowed groggily into her pillow again. Outside, the coyotes were up to their old tricks, howling and yipping at the moon, even though there was barely a moon to yip at. She flipped onto her back again and stared in frustration at the ceiling. Wondered if going totally decaf was the solution to her constantly interrupted sleep.

She'd been a light sleeper since David died, and it had been two years now. Two years of listening to the wind in the trees and the coyotes on the hill. Two years of making dinner for one.

Two years of running their campground business on her own.

She felt the emptiness of missing him again. Losing him had been so terrible at first. If it hadn't been for her faith in God and the comfort she found in prayer, she might have packed her bags and joined her family in Virginia. But the business had been David's dream, and he'd awakened every morning, eager to embrace it again. She couldn't walk away from something that had been so important to him.

A strange, metallic sound broke her thoughts, and Rachel stilled. Cocked an ear…listened for a moment.

There it was again.

And again.

Throwing back her floral comforter, she strode to the long window facing the strip of land she'd recently acquired. The skimpy moon and woods were swimming in fog making it difficult to see, but—

A jolt of adrenaline hit her as Rachel spotted the moving beam of a flashlight in the misty darkness. Someone was out there! And so was the expensive ground-moving machinery the Decker brothers had parked there late yesterday afternoon.

Grabbing her robe from the foot of the bed and pulling it over her dorm shirt, she hurried across the hardwood to the hall, then through the living room to her kitchen. The light below the over-the-range microwave shone dimly, but it was enough illumination to locate the heavy-duty flashlight under the sink. Snagging it, she unlocked the patio door to her elevated deck and strode, barefooted, to the redwood railing.

The intruder's light went out.

Rachel shone her beam down through the darkness and fog—flicked it over tree limbs that were almost fully leafed—found the mist-shrouded bulldozer, rock crusher and dump truck fifty yards away.

A new rush of adrenaline hit her when the beam revealed a hooded figure crouched near the dump truck. "Hey!" she shouted. "What are you doing out there?"

The figure bolted—clicked his light back on and crashed down through the thick hemlocks and oaks toward the creek below. But not before Rachel caught another glimpse of him.

Rushing inside, she flipped through the phone book, found the number for Charity, Pennsylvania's tiny police force and punched it in. Chirpy night dispatcher and church organist, Emma Lucille Bridger, answered. Rachel and Emma Lu were kindred spirits of sorts. They were both avid readers and borderline insomniacs. Even though it was common knowledge that the sixty-seven-year-old dispatcher napped during her shift, no one on the force minded. Her only job was to answer the phone.

"Emma Lu, it's Rachel Patterson at the campground. I'm trying not to be an alarmist, but someone's prowling around outside my house."

Emma Lucille's sweet soprano rose, and her grandmotherly instincts kicked in. "Are you okay, Rachel?"

"Yes, I'm fine. I'm just worried about— Emma Lu, Decker Construction parked some equipment here yesterday. I'm afraid it might have been vandalized."

Emma Lu spoke quickly. "Okay, honey, I'll radio Fish and tell him to get down to your place right away. He's on patrol, so it might take him a few minutes. You sit tight now. Don't you go outside."

"I won't," Rachel agreed, meaning it. She'd already done that, and going outside to check on someone who obviously didn't want to be seen wasn't the smartest thing she'd ever done. "Thanks, Emma Lu."

"You're welcome. Just stay safe."

She'd just finished pulling on jeans, sneakers and a navy sweatshirt, when she heard the not-too-distant rumble of a vehicle. Her pulse picked up speed. It was after 2:00 a.m., and her campground was five miles from Charity. It was too soon for Patrolman Larry "Fish" Troutman's arrival.

Striding to the window facing her driveway, Rachel cupped her hands against the glass. Headlights poked through the blanket of fog, then followed the winding lane past her camp store and tourist cabins. From Memorial Day weekend through Pennsylvania's deer hunting season, light poles lit the way, but the holiday was still almost three weeks off—and the breaker for the lights was in the camp store.

The motion lights at the corners of her wood-sided ranch house clicked on. And Rachel's anxiety dissolved when a green truck with a Pennsylvania Game Commission emblem on the door swung in beside her red Explorer and parked.

Startled to see him at this hour, but unable to stop the happy quickening of her pulse, Rachel tossed her fingertips through her straight sable bangs and shaggy cap cut—then went stone-still with guilt. Guilt and another emotion it shamed her to acknowledge.

Gathering her composure, she stepped outside to greet her unexpected visitor.

The early-May temperatures had been cool until yesterday when they reached the low seventies. Now, according to the round outdoor thermometer wired to the deck railing, it had dipped twenty degrees. A faint breeze ruffled the trees, carrying with it the fog-damp fragrances of earth, pine and fallen leaves.

"Jake?" she said when he'd exited his vehicle. "What are you doing here?"

He kept his voice low, but she could hear the concern in it. "I was driving back from a callout when your call came over the radio. Are you all right?"

"I'm fine," she returned, warmed by his concern despite her feelings of disloyalty. "Just a little on edge."

Wildlife conservation officer Jake Campbell started up the flight of six steps, his dark brown hair attractively mussed. For a big man, he had a loose, confident way of moving and chiseled good looks that were a little grim until he smiled. He had good eyes, too, Rachel thought. Perceptive brown eyes that missed nothing. The dark green uniform jacket hanging open over his black T-shirt and jeans nearly concealed the sidearm on his hip.

"So what happened here tonight?" he asked when he'd reached her. "The dispatcher said something about a prowler and vandalism."

She nodded. "The prowler part's correct. Vandalism's only a possibility right now." She backtracked to bring him up to speed. "When we spoke last, I think I mentioned putting in a mini golf course on the strip of land I acquired a few months ago. A little putt-putt for the kids."

"Yeah, you did."

She indicated the foggy clearing beyond the trees. "Yesterday, Tim Decker dropped off his equipment because he'll be leveling the land in the morning. He said it would be fine sitting there. Then a few minutes ago, I heard noises and went outside. Someone with a flashlight was messing around near Tim's truck." She paused. "When I yelled, he took off into the woods."

Jake's features lined and he sighed. "Rachel, you're alone here. You should have stayed inside and called the police immediately."

"I know. I thought of that after the fact." But the past two years had forced her to become independent—and part of her liked it. "If David had been here, he would have handled it. But he isn't, so it's my job."

Jake didn't comment, but the troubled look in his eyes sent a clear message: He didn't *like* that it was her job. "Did you get a good look at him?"

"Not really, considering the fog. But I know he was white, and he was wearing a dark hooded jacket with a light-colored emblem on the back of it." She stilled as her mind re-created that split-second happening, then spoke hesitantly. "He was carrying something. Something light-colored that flapped when he ran. A bag, maybe."

"If it was a bag, that says he expected to carry something away. Do you know if Decker left tools or anything portable behind?"

"I'm not sure. I hope not."

Another set of headlights pierced the darkness and fog. This time, the vehicle was a black-and-white police cruiser, and the patrolman who got out was a tall, lanky young man in his mid-twenties with fire-red hair and a mouth full of silver braces. Fish was the youngest member of the department, and the one with the least experience. The thud of the cruiser's door closing sounded hollow in the stillness.

"Hey, Rachel," he said solemnly as he ascended the steps. "Emma Lu said you had some uninvited company tonight. You okay?"

"Yes, I'm fine," she assured him as he reached her. "Fish, have you met Jake Campbell? Jake's—"

"The new W.C.O.," Fish said cordially, clasping the hand Jake extended. "Our paths cross from time to time. Nice to see you again, Jake."

"Same here, Fish."

"You live around here?"

Rachel nearly smiled. It was a casual inquiry, but

Fish obviously wondered why Jake was here at two-thirty in the morning. The amusement in Jake's eyes told her he'd caught that unspoken question, too.

"About a mile up the road," he replied. "I was coming home from a callout when I heard your dispatcher on the radio. Thought I'd see if my neighbor needed some help."

Apparently satisfied with the answer, he smiled his approval and pulled out a notebook and pen. "Okay, Rachel, let's take it from the top. First, can you give me a description of the guy? If it was a guy."

Rachel told him everything she could remember, glad that Fish was on duty. With the Charity P.D. being small, there was a chance the new police chief would have responded. She'd only spoken to Lon Perris once since he'd pinned on the badge—the night of his welcoming dinner sponsored by the chamber of commerce. But she hadn't come away from that conversation feeling warm and fuzzy. Chief Perris was... She searched for a word Reverend Landers would approve of. "Condescending" was the best she could do.

When she'd finished detailing what had happened, Fish made a final note, then tucked his pen and pad away. "Okay, I'll take a look at the site and drive around the loops before I leave—make sure this guy isn't coming back for a vehicle. You're pretty far off the beaten path, so I doubt he got here on foot." He chewed his lip. "You didn't hear any engine sounds before Jake got here, right?"

"No."

"Jake? See any vehicles on the road tonight?"

Jake wandered closer, his boots quiet on the plank floor. And Rachel felt another stir of attraction as she looked up at him. "No, and I was watching for them. But I came in from the other direction, not from town. Since the guy cut through the woods, he might have parked on one of the logging roads."

"Yeah, he probably did." Fish pulled a flashlight from a loop on his belt, then shone it in a wide arc over the construction site and campground. "Could have been a kid looking to siphon gas or steal tools. It's a little early in the season for that stuff, but it happens."

He tucked the light away and turned back to Rachel. "Like I said, I'll check out the sites and loops, but it's kind of hard to see now. I'll be back in the morning for a better look, okay?"

"That'd be great," she returned. "Thanks for coming. I know I should have told Emma to hold off sending you down here until daybreak, but I wanted to report the incident right away in case there are damages."

"No problem," he said, heading for the steps. He stopped then and glanced back. "One more thing. That logo or whatever it was on the back of the jacket? Can you describe it?"

Rachel hesitated. As descriptions went, it wasn't the best. "It looked like a round head with rabbit ears. That's probably not very helpful, but I only saw it for a second."

"It's a start," Fish replied. He started down the steps, his lanky body still half-turned toward her. "I'll stop back if I find anything out of the ordinary. Otherwise, I'll see you in the morning."

"Thanks, Fish."

"Yep. Night, Jake."

"Night, Fish."

And in short order, the cruiser's red taillights had

disappeared, leaving her alone with Jake again. Rachel looked up at him. She was more attuned to his presence now that they were alone, more attuned to their woodsy isolation.

"I should get moving, too," he said with some hesitance. "Will you be okay? Do you want to call someone to stay with you?"

"I'll be all right," she replied. "I'm a lot tougher than I look."

A faint smile tipped his lips. "So I've noticed. You paint, you plow snow, you run a successful business and you even make a decent cup of coffee. I'm impressed."

"Don't be," she said, smiling. "It's all smoke and mirrors."

"No, it isn't," he returned. "It's all you." Then out of the blue, the night seemed to shrink around them, his gaze softened and he looked at her in a way no man had looked at her since David. "You're an extraordinary woman, Rachel."

For a few seconds, she didn't even breathe—and she wasn't alone. Jake seemed just as stunned by his words as she was. Then he quickly rebounded and spoke again, his tone a little gruff.

"Well, I'm out of here. Maggie's probably wondering why she's still in her pen." He drew a breath. "If there's another problem, and you're not sure it's serious enough to call Fish, I'm only a phone call away."

Rachel found a smile somewhere, but her heart was still racing. "Thanks. And thank you for checking up on me."

He sent her a tight-lipped nod. "Just being a good

neighbor." His brow lined then, and he glanced toward the construction site. "Make sure you lock up, okay?"

"I will. Good night."

Rachel waited until his vehicle, too, had been swallowed by the fog, then went back inside and shoved the lock into place. Her pretty hunter green-and-burgundy kitchen was ablaze with light, warm and welcoming. But she was far from relaxed. She and Jake had developed a comfortable friendship since he'd transferred from Potter County to the valley last November. Shortly afterward, he and his Irish setter had started showing up at her camp store. Several times over the winter, he'd even plowed the campground's incredibly long driveway before she could get David's snowblower out of the utility shed. Now…now their friendship was changing. She couldn't deny her attraction to him. What woman with a beating pulse and decent vision could? But she'd loved only one man in her life, and she'd loved him with all of her heart. This felt…

Wrong? a tiny voice in her head asked.

"No," she whispered. "And it should."

Jake clicked on his low beams and drove deeper into the mist, his nerves on edge. What had happened back there? And what had possessed him to say something so totally idiotic? The second the words left his lips, he'd felt the hairs at the nape of his neck stand on end. She was beautiful and smart, and so many other things. But the widow Patterson was still grieving, and he wasn't looking. Not after Heather trashed his dreams and took a sledge hammer to their future. No, he wasn't looking for anything more than friendship, some pleasant conversation and, occasionally, a good cup of coffee—maybe one of her chocolate chip cookies. She liked to bake.

He followed the winding lane to the highway, waved to Fish who'd just exited one of the side loops, then turned right and headed for home. He snapped off the radio when Hank Williams's twangy "Your Cheating Heart" flowed from the speakers. He didn't need a musical reminder. The stack of bills he'd paid for the November wedding that hadn't happened was reminder enough.

A pregnant cow elk that looked mere minutes from delivering lumbered out of the fog and crossed the road. Jake touched the toe of his boot to the brake. He managed a smile. It was birthing time in the Pennsylvania wilds—which seemed to be happening a week ahead of time this year. Other wildlife conservation officers had already reported seeing a few calves. Unusual, but calving time generally occurred when the most nutritious food was available, and they'd had an early spring.

The commonwealth's huge elk herd was approaching seven hundred here and in neighboring counties, and drew visitors from all over, especially in the late summer to early fall when the bulls were bugling and gathering their harems. Rachel had mentioned that she did a booming business then.

Pretty, shocked-by-his-words Rachel who would always love her husband with a quiet devotion Jake would never know. Never even glimpse. But that was life, wasn't it?

Suddenly a vehicle shot past him in the opposite direction. Glad for the distraction, Jake made a U-turn in the middle of the road and hit the gas. The dated SUV had two people in front, and as he gained on it, he tried to make out the license plate. Even if one of them was Rachel's night visitor, Jake couldn't stop them; he had no authority. He *could* get some information for Fish, though. They hit a stretch of road where the guardrails seemed to pin back the fog.

He clicked on his high beams—and quickly recognized young Marty Miller's beat-up beige Cherokee. Then he dropped his gaze to the brand-new vanity plate on the back of it and rolled his eyes. RD HNTR. *Road Hunter.*

It took only a few moments for Jake and his gut to decide that twenty-something Marty wasn't Rachel's 2:00 a.m. trespasser. He'd talked to the kid a few times, and while Marty seemed to enjoy grinning it up and waving red flags at authority figures, he wasn't the clandestine type.

Clicking on his low beams again, Jake put some space between their vehicles, then smiled at the mocking license plate. Kids.

When he got to the only red light on Main Street, he pulled into the left turning lane beside the driver and put his window down. Marty did the same. "Nice plates," Jake called.

The kid with the bushel basket-size mass of brown curls smiled. "Thanks. Just got 'em."

Jake smiled back. "You weren't doing anything you shouldn't out there tonight, were you? Like spotting the fields looking for newborns?"

Miller glanced at the cute blonde beside him. "Nah, I wasn't grocery shopping. Even if I wanted to—which I don't—she wouldn't let me. She likes the babies."

"Good. Now you should get her home before her dad comes looking for you."

"Don't have to," the kid returned in a cheeky voice. "She has her own place. Her dad doesn't know she's still out."

"Yeah? He'll know if I tell him."

Laughing again, the kid waved, raised his window and drove off.

Nice kid, Jake decided. But if he caught him hunting from his car, he'd still fine his scrawny butt.

Slowly, barely crawling along, the vehicle left one of the rutted logging roads lacing the woods, only dim parking lights illuminating the way. A large cloth bag and shovel lay in the backseat. Nervous thoughts zinged through a mind too rattled to think clearly. How much had Rachel Patterson seen? Was the hood and fog enough to obscure her view? What to do? What to do? A small, jittery voice whispered that the only solution was to leave Charity. A louder one shouted, *No! Not when things are finally working out.*

Unquestionably, the second voice was right. The idea of leaving Charity was nearly as disturbing as the thought of a prison term. He commanded himself to think. He had to delay that construction project or risk losing everything. Sugar in the diesel tanks wouldn't work…and the tires were too thick to slash and too easily replaced. If only he'd heard about Rachel's plans sooner than yesterday.

Gripping the steering wheel, he exhaled a blast of frustration. With construction starting tomorrow, his only recourse was to go back and try again.

Or was it?

A dark thought rose, then twisted and turned and

became increasingly darker. He began to tremble, felt sweat bead his upper lip. No! No, that was a last resort.

He had to go back.

TWO

Rachel jerked awake the next morning at seven-fifteen to sunshine and the growl of construction equipment flowing through the screen in her bedroom window. She leaped out of bed and dressed. The machines were already leveling the ground, so that meant there'd been no damage to the equipment, thank the Lord. But she'd still wanted to greet Tim when he arrived, and explain what had happened last night.

She'd just shut off her coffeemaker when someone rapped at her patio door. Crossing the kitchen, she opened her hunter green vertical blinds to see Jake standing on her deck. Feeling a burst of nerves that seemed to double her heart rate, she slid open the glass pane and screen.

"Good morning," she said. "I would have thought you'd be sleeping in today after being up half the night."

He stepped into the kitchen. "Nope. My mom phoned a while ago and woke me up." He paused. "As for getting more sack time—I could say the same about you. You probably got less sleep than I did." This morning he wore jeans, a dark green T-shirt that hugged his broad shoulders and, for a change, not boots but running shoes. His dark hair was still damp from his shower, and the clean smell of citrus clung to his skin.

His voice softened. "I just came by to see if you were all right. I figured you'd be up because the guys were starting work at seven."

That warm feeling in her chest blossomed but soon gave way to jitters. Maybe because this was the first time he'd been inside her home and he seemed to fill the room. Or maybe because she was so aware of him filling it. He towered over her, seven or eight inches taller than her five-feet-six. She slid the screen shut. "I'm good. As I said last night, I'm a lot tougher than I look."

"But you still had trouble getting back to sleep," he guessed.

"Sad but true." He knew about her sleepless nights. They'd talked about them. "But I dug out my iPod, and listened to a new CD I'd downloaded. That helped."

"Casey Kasem's top forty?"

She smiled. "No, moody oboes and ocean waves. Top forty for insomniacs." When his rugged features lined in sympathy, she felt another rash of nerves. She gestured toward her round oak table and chairs. "Have a seat. Can I get you a cup of coffee?"

"Yeah, thanks, if you're having some. But I can't stay long. I have to get back and dress for work. I'm giving a talk to the kids at the elementary school this morning."

"About?"

"Respecting wildlife, the necessity for hunter safety courses…that kind of thing. What's on your agenda today?"

"After I deliver coffee to Tim and his crew, I'm

headed to town. I have a hundred things to do before I go to the nursing home." During the off-season, she occasionally helped out in the activities room. It gave her something to do, and made her feel good at the same time. That would change soon with the campground opening.

"Since we're both on the clock, do you care if we take our coffee outside? At the risk of looking like a stereotype, I wouldn't mind walking over to see how the ground moving's going."

Good idea. She'd be more comfortable out there. "Sure. Just give me a second, then we can go." She pulled brown stoneware mugs and a stainless steel thermos from her oak cabinets. "Actually, I should have seen Tim before this. My insomniac's top forty worked so well that I overslept this morning, and didn't have a chance to tell him about my late-night visi—"

Heavy footsteps on the deck stairs stopped her in mid-sentence, and a second later, a beefy man in a plaid flannel shirt and jeans appeared at the screen door. Beneath his salt-and-pepper crew cut, Tim Decker's deep-set gray eyes couldn't have been colder.

Rachel strode to the door—opened the screen. "Tim?"

"Sorry," he said. "We're shut down, and I don't know for how long."

Her pulse quickened as she realized that those engine sounds had ceased. "What happened?"

"Someone punched holes in my dozer's oil and transmission filters. If we'd noticed, we could've replaced them. But we fired up the dozer, put it to work and ran every last drop of fluid out of it. Froze it up solid."

Rachel felt sick. If she'd gotten up earlier, she could

have told him what had happened last night, and he would have checked his equipment. This wouldn't have happened.

Jake's gaze hardened. "Unbelievable."

"Yeah," Decker said. "The freak tried to puncture the fuel tank on my truck, too, but couldn't get through the thick wall." His gaze shifted to Rachel again. "Okay if I use your land line? I gotta report this, and there's no cell service this far from town."

"Of course," she replied nervously, then followed him to the kitchen's wall phone. "But before you do that there's something you should know. There was a—a disturbance here around two this morning. I called the station, and Fish drove down to check things out."

Tim pivoted abruptly, the stunned look on his face quickly turning to anger. "Are you telling me you knew about this?"

Jake stepped between them. "Calm down. I was here in the middle of the night, too. None of us knew your dozer'd been sabotaged. That includes Fish. You need to let Rachel explain."

The officer who answered Tim Decker's call wasn't a friendly redhead with a mouthful of silver. The rip cord–thin man who got out of the black-and-white cruiser had piercing eyes, a square jaw and a severe buzz cut. Chief Lon Perris wore a gray uniform shirt, black pants and tie, and an almost smothering air of authority. Thirty years after the fact, his lean cheeks still bore the scars from teenage acne.

Jake and Rachel left their coffee mugs on the deck stairs where they'd been sitting and walked out to meet him. Too agitated to sit and wait, Tim was rechecking his equipment.

Charity's chief of police position had seen major turnovers in the past year. First John Wilcox had died, elevating Rachel's friend Margo to acting chief, then when Margo and her husband Cole started their private investigations firm, Brett Johnson had accepted the post. Now Brett was in law school, and Lon Perris, a quickly hired, unknown commodity from the Philadelphia area wore the badge. It was like a game of musical chairs. Hum a few bars, stop short and Charity had a new lawman at the helm.

Perris shut the cruiser's door, gave Rachel a rude once-over that made her go still, then shook hands with Jake and introduced himself. "Chief of Police Lon Perris. You Tim Decker?"

Jake slid Rachel a what's-with-this-guy? look before he answered. "No, Jake Campbell. Tim's over at the site."

Perris glanced through the trees and tall grasses where Decker stood with his two-man crew, then addressed Jake—not Rachel—again. "Which one's Decker?"

Rachel watched Jake's eyes narrow, and visible lines of tension crease his brow. "Decker's the big guy in the flannel shirt," he said coolly. "And you should be talking to Rachel. This is her property, not mine."

If Jake's brusque tone surprised him, Perris didn't let on.

Deciding that one of them should be polite, Rachel stepped forward and spoke amicably. "You probably don't remember me, Chief. We met at the—"

"Yes, the chamber's dinner. I know who you are,

Mrs. Patterson, and we'll be talking. But at the moment, Mr. Decker is my main priority." He started away. "I trust you'll stay available."

He trusted that she'd stay available? In the back of her mind, a tiny voice whispered the latest message posted outside the church: Remember, he who angers you controls you. The words fell on deaf ears. "I'll be here until nine-thirty if you have any questions," she replied. "After that, I'm afraid we'll have to make other arrangements."

"That'll be fine," he said without turning around. Then he continued on through the trampled-grass path leading to the construction site.

Rachel stormed over to her redwood steps where Jake sat, cradling his coffee mug between the spread of his legs. She dropped down beside him. Strangely, even as irritated as she was, she couldn't overlook the obvious. He was a big, attractive, well-built man, and he looked good sitting on her steps. Almost as though he belonged there.

"Ignore him," Jake said. "He's not worth your time. The man's a dyed-in-the-wool chauvinist with zero respect for women."

"Did I say I was upset?"

"You didn't have to," he returned with a faint grin. "The flames shooting out of your nostrils spoke volumes."

Rachel accepted the coffee mug he handed her. "Sorry. Apparently, I get grumpy when I'm shunned." She took a sip. "But the man got so far under my skin that I was afraid I'd have to see a surgeon." She met his amused brown eyes. Then she smiled, too—until a subtle wave of tension moved between them, and she had to look away.

"Do you ever wonder what makes people like Perris tick?" she asked, masking her uneasiness. "What possesses someone to be deliberately rude?"

Something in Jake's tone told her he'd felt that brief connection, too. It was a hesitance—something she couldn't put a name to. "Hard telling. Basic unhappiness? Lousy upbringing? No social skills? We've all dealt with people like that."

"Not like him."

"No?"

"No," she repeated. "Most people I come in contact with are pretty decent. They say, 'Hello,' they say, 'Have a nice day,' and they don't give women dismissive looks. Then there's the lovely Mr. Perris."

"Count your blessings. At least with Perris, what you see is what you get. He doesn't pretend to be something he's not. Some people—" Jake's tone cooled. "Some people are so good at hiding their feelings that it takes months to see who they really are. Even then, you can't be sure you're on point."

The knowledge that he was no longer talking about Perris landed with a thud, and Rachel's uneasiness faded. She glanced at him again. When he'd first arrived, they'd talked like all new neighbors do. Nothing personal—just everyday chitchat that had led her to ask if he had a family. He'd joked that he'd been engaged once, but luckily his head had cleared before he'd taken that trip to the altar. Is that what he'd been referring to? she wondered. His broken engagement? And was that hurt or anger she'd heard in his voice?

"Jake?"

Flashing a smile that never reached his eyes, he stood, drained his coffee and stepped down to the ground. "Sorry. We'll have to continue this stimulating conversation another time. I need to change for work, and you have things to do in town."

He handed her his cup. Then, as though he'd done it dozens of times before, he surprised her by taking her hand and easing her up from the step, bringing them eye-to-eye. Rachel drew a soft breath. His sun-warmed hand was broad and tanned, and after a brief moment, she took hers back. He started for home.

"Have a good morning."

"You, too," she said, her emotions warring with her sense of propriety. Despite the pangs of guilt she couldn't ignore, she liked him. She honestly liked him. And lifting her chin, she told herself there was nothing wrong with that. Nothing at all.

But ten minutes later when she entered the living room to turn on the morning news, David smiled at her from their gold-framed wedding photograph, and tears welled in her eyes.

Holy Savior Elder Care was set on beautifully landscaped grounds, the low, white brick building ablaze with bright yellow forsythias, vibrant greenery and red and yellow tulips. Ringed with more spring flowers, a snow-white statue of Jesus sitting with children at his knee rested on a raised platform before the wood-framed double-door entrance.

Jake crossed the parking lot and went inside, asked for directions, then proceeded past pink-and-green floral wallpaper to the activities room. He spotted Rachel at one of the tables, chatting with two elderly women who were cutting coupons from newspaper supplements. At the front of the room, other residents worked on puzzles or watched a rerun of *Little House on the Prairie*. He stopped just short of the doorway, feeling conspicuous in his uniform.

Rachel glanced up in surprise, beckoned another volunteer over to take her place, then strode into the hall to meet him.

"Jake?" she said, slightly alarmed. "Is something wrong?"

"No. Not wrong, exactly. But I was having an early lunch at the diner with some friends, and Perris came in." He glanced around. The hall had gotten busy with visitors and nurses aides wheeling residents to other venues. "Can we talk somewhere else? I know you're busy. I won't keep you long."

"Of course. Let me talk to Gail—she's the activities director—then I'll see you outside."

A few minutes later, he watched her breeze through the home's double doors. Sunlight glanced off the small gold cross she wore with tiny gold earrings, a white knit top and deep purple chinos. Trying to ignore the uninvited change in his pulse, Jake joined her on the sidewalk and reminded himself he was only here to make a pitch for protection. Nothing more. No matter how beautiful she looked.

They fell into step together, strolling past bright yellow goldfinches pecking seeds from multilevel feeders

"So what's up?" Rachel asked. "What did Perris tell you?"

Jake glanced down at her. "He said your visitor

had to have made a second trip back to your place last night."

"I know. He mentioned that to me before he left. He said the light 'chinking' sounds I heard earlier weren't consistent with someone banging a screwdriver into a fuel tank." She glanced up at him. "Did he tell you that whoever damaged Tim's dozer got the hammer and screwdriver from Decker's own toolbox?"

"Yeah, he did."

She sighed. "I'm not sure I like someone coming and going at will on my property."

"I'm not wild about it, either," Jake said gravely. "Which brings me to the reason I'm here. When Perris said the guy came back, your living alone in the woods really started to bother me. I think you should get a dog."

"A *dog?*"

He had to smile. He liked the way her sable bangs just missed colliding with her dark eyelashes, liked her sea-green eyes. "Yeah, a dog. They look a lot like Maggie—four legs and a lot of fur. Good ones bark up a storm when their owners are threatened."

The little lift he felt when she grinned took a sudden nosedive.

"David loved dogs—big, slurpy breeds. And we did consider getting one for a time. But we worried that a big dog and our guests might not be a good mix."

Jake looked away for an instant—told himself that Rachel's mentioning David wasn't any big deal. "Then you get a smaller, even-tempered dog with a big bark."

"Maybe someday," she said. "But I don't see the need right now. The man I saw last night was angry at Tim, not me." She glanced toward the home's entrance, then brought her pretty gaze back to him. "Was there…something else?"

Annoyed with himself, he shook his head. Now she probably thought he'd made a special trip to talk to her, when he could have phoned or stopped at the campground later. "No, that's it. I just thought I'd drop in because I had to pass the nursing home anyway."

"Oh. Well, thank you." She consulted her wristwatch, and the sun glanced off the gold wedding band on her finger. "I'd better get back inside now, though. It's almost lunchtime, and some of my friends need help with their food."

With the workload waiting for her at the campground, she still took time to help others. He liked that about her. But today he wouldn't tell her she was fabulous—or whatever idiotic word he'd used last night that made them both uncomfortable. "I have to go, too. But think about what I said."

"I'll do that. Thanks again."

Brushing off her thanks, he headed for his vehicle. "No problem. Friends are supposed to look out for each other."

Friends, he thought, getting his head straight as he started the green game-commission truck and pulled back onto the road. That's what they were, and what he was comfortable with. He could do a lot worse.

At two o'clock, Rachel drove down into her wooded campground to see Nate Carter's yellow company truck parked beside her white-sided camp store. Sunlight flashed off two long silver canisters in the truck's bed, both secured by steel framing. She swung in beside him as Nate got out of his vehicle.

Nate was a compact man about her height with light brown hair, dated steel-rimmed aviator glasses and a nice smile. A denim jacket stitched with his company name—Carter Propane Sales—topped his jeans and chambray shirt, but on Sundays, he was a suit-and-tie man all the way.

"Afternoon," he called, walking around the truck to meet her.

"Afternoon," she called back. "Have you been here long?"

"Just a few minutes. I was making deliveries in the area and stopped to see if you needed to have your tanks filled." He wiggled an empty foam cup before dropping it in the nearby trash receptacle. "I was also hoping for a cup of coffee and some scintillating conversation."

Laughing and choosing a key from her ring, Rachel ascended the wide wooden stoop, opened the white screen door and inserted her key in the lock. "If you're looking for 'scintillating,' you've come to the wrong place, but coffee's doable." She stepped inside, and he followed. "As for my tanks, I haven't checked the gauges yet, but I'm probably low."

"You are," he admitted sheepishly. "I had some time to kill before you got here." He stepped around three waist-high stacks of cartons on the floor. "You're under twenty percent at your house. Camp store's just a little better than that."

Rachel dropped her keys on the blue counter separating her galley from the store, then slipped behind the bar to start her small coffeemaker. The large dispenser would be pressed into service when her guests began piling in.

"Well, then, let's fill them." She put a filter pack of coffee in the basket, added a dash of salt and turned on the unit. "How's tomorrow for you?"

"Tomorrow's good. Morning or afternoon?"

Rachel carried two white mugs to the counter where Nate had commandeered a stool. "Come anytime. It doesn't matter. I'll be here all day."

"Great. I'll stop by in the morning. Jillian has a hair appointment around three, so if my afternoon's free, I can tag along. Maybe take her out afterward for an early dinner."

"Can't imagine her saying no to that," Rachel returned, smiling.

"Yeah, she'll like that." He paused for a moment as the rich aroma of coffee brewing spiced the air, and steaming, spitting coffee dripped into the carafe. A sly twinkle rose in his eyes when Rachel took the stool beside him. "So," he said far too innocently, "anything new going on in your neck of the woods?"

She had to laugh. So that's why he'd waited for her. He'd heard. Some days she swore the number of police scanners in Charity outnumbered the population. "Let me guess, you have a scanner."

"No, I ran into Emma Lucille at the Quick Mart early this morning. She'd just turned over the dispatcher's desk to Sarah. You know Charity. On a slow day, somebody's hangnail is big news."

That was an understatement.

"Anyway, Emma Lu was talking to Ben Caruthers from the hardware store, who apparently *does* have a scanner, and they were discussing your prowler. Ben was really champing at the bit for information—wanted to know if Fish had made an arrest."

"Well, if you heard her answer, you know he didn't. And technically, the guy was Tim Decker's prowler. Apparently, Tim's not one of his favorite people."

"Apparently." Nate's broad face lined in concern. "Rachel," he began hesitantly, "I know this is none of my business, but...do you have a gun?"

"A gun?" she repeated.

He hurried to explain himself. "Only for your protection. What if this guy thinks you recognized him? You're miles from help if you need it."

First Jake's suggestion that she get a dog, now this. God had been good to her. He'd blessed her with wonderful friends...and one very caring neighbor. "Nate, I appreciate your concern, but really, who would risk killing someone over an act of vandalism? We're not talking about the mob here."

"I know that, but you're alone," he said, pressing his point. "Non-mob things happen. Now if you want a gun—"

"No way." Rising, she retrieved the coffee carafe and returned to fill their cups. "A gun in the hand of someone who's never used one is a surefire recipe for disaster." She reached under the counter for a basket filled with stir sticks and sugar and creamer packets. "Now let's talk about something uplifting. Something that will put a smile on my face."

Still troubled but seeming to know that she wouldn't change her mind, he conceded. "Okay, like what?"

Rachel laughed. "Well, you could tell me that my propane will be cheaper this year."

* * *

Maggie crashed into the woods after another chipmunk, and with a sharp whistle, Jake called her back and slowed his run. The sun was sliding toward the horizon, but the day was still warm, full of the smells, sights and sounds of spring. Every bird in the valley was out doing what birds did, and seemingly overnight, grassy fields had become endless carpets of dandelions.

He wiped his face with a hand towel, jammed it into his back pocket, then settled into a cool-down jog. He paused to listen outside Rachel's camp store. Music. Somewhere on the property, country singer Alan Jackson was recalling coming of age on the Chattahoochee. Jake followed the song to the bathhouses—and Rachel. She'd propped the door open with a rock, and low sunlight shone through it, highlighting her face-framing sable hair as she slapped mint green paint on a wall. She looked young and industrious in cutoff jeans and a yellow T-shirt.

She whirled around in surprise when Maggie dashed past him and bolted inside to say hello, her toenails clicking on the concrete floor. "Three visits in one day?" she said, laughing and scrubbing her fingers through the setter's silky coat. "You two are going to spoil me."

Jake worked up a smile. That's what he'd been afraid of. Not the spoiling part. He was worried about sending the wrong message. He didn't want her thinking what women probably thought when a man made three trips to see them in one day. He was here only because his house felt empty, he'd put in a full day, and he was—as his grandmother used to say—at loose ends.

Rachel took in his navy cutoffs and white tank top. "Out for a run?"

"Just a short one. I was about to head for home when I heard the music and thought I'd see what you were up to."

She had amazing eyes. Eyes that saw too much, he decided, recalling the conversation he'd put a stop to this morning. He knew he'd piqued her interest. But no man with an ounce of pride admitted to a beautiful woman—even one who still wore a wedding band—that his fiancée had preferred someone else to him.

He glanced around at Rachel's handiwork. "Looks good." The bathhouse was constructed of cement blocks, smooth now under countless coats of paint. Above white fixtures, a long, wood-framed mirror was bolted to the wall, while the opposite wall hosted freshly painted shower stalls. "Got another brush? I'll help you finish."

"Thanks, but I only have one wall to go." Rachel dipped to scoop a rag from the floor, then wiped her brush and walked toward him. She was long and lithe, grace in motion on two white-sneakered feet. "I was ready to call it a day anyway. Give me a minute to seal the paint can and clean my brush, then we can walk up to the store. You and Maggie look like you could use a cold drink—and I know I could use one."

"Sounds good," he said. "But I'm buying."

They didn't stay at the camp store; they walked. The store was too warm, and the sunset was too vibrant to miss. In a while, they found themselves sipping Pepsi from plastic bottles near the site of last night's vandalism. The twilight song of the peepers filled the air, Alan Jackson's boyhood reminiscing long gone.

Rachel glanced at the partially chewed-up earth and lone piece of equipment and once again felt a twinge of guilt over the dozer's damage when it was in her care.

Jake spoke. "Looks like Decker moved his other equipment before it could suffer a similar fate."

Rachel nodded. "Chief Perris suggested it, but Tim had already decided to move them until they were ready to resume work. He's sending a flatbed for the bulldozer tomorrow."

"Nothing from the police yet?"

"No, but the way Perris feels about me—make that women in general—I'm not expecting a call."

Rachel watched him take another swig of his Pepsi, then screw the cap back on. "I have a favor to ask."

A favor? "Since I can't imagine you asking anything I wouldn't say yes to…sure. What do you need?"

"I'd like you to invite Maggie to a slumber party."

She cocked her head. "You want me to keep your dog overnight?"

"Yeah, I do. I have a meeting in Harrisburg first thing tomorrow morning. I could drive down there at the crack of dawn, but I'd rather leave tonight." He pinned his gaze on the dark pines and leafy maples lining the road ahead. "Naturally, I explained to her that she'd be fine in her pen, but after hearing about your prowler… Well, weird as it sounds, Maggie said she's afraid to stay alone."

Rachel smiled, a lovely warmth enveloping her. He wasn't concerned about Maggie, he was concerned about her. "Maybe you should tell Maggie that she has nothing to be afraid of. Now that the nasty man has accomplished his nasty deed, there's no reason for him to come back."

As if to punctuate his point, Maggie crashed out of the darkening woods and undergrowth, her golden-red fur wet after a splash through the creek below. She circled her good-looking master, then nuzzled his hand until he reached down to scratch behind her ear. But his gaze never left Rachel's.

"You're probably right," he said, straightening. "Chances are he won't come back, but I still wish you'd keep her. She wouldn't be any trouble. She could sleep on your deck."

"Jake—"

Briefly touching a finger to her lips, he softened his voice. "Before you refuse again, maybe I should tell you something. I've mentioned my younger brother Greg to you before, haven't I?"

Rachel searched his face. "Yes."

His dark gaze clouded. "Once upon a time we had a sister."

THREE

Had. They'd *had* a sister. Past tense.

"Tell me," she said quietly.

He took a second to gather his thoughts, then began. "One summer night, Carrie and two of her friends were walking home from the library—something they'd done dozens of times before. It wasn't quite dark, and we lived in a safe neighborhood. So as everyone said later, there was no need for our parents to worry."

But there was a need, Rachel realized, and a feeling of dread settled over her.

"That night, Carrie and Erin dropped Liza off at her house, then half a block from ours, Carrie said good-night to Erin and headed home." He paused and his brow furrowed. "She'd just turned sixteen. She was pretty and smart, and she wanted to be a fashion designer. She drew all the time." He blew out a breath. "They never caught the man who raped her. She died from a blow to the head during the assault."

Rachel didn't know what to say for a moment, then murmured a time-worn response that never really said enough. "Jake, I'm so sorry. How old were you when Carrie died?"

"I was her big brother by three minutes."

Twins. That seemed to make losing her even worse. They'd begun life together, were born together—learned to walk and talk together. How many times had he wished he'd been with her that night? Rachel wondered. Big brothers were supposed to look after their baby sisters—keep them from harm. But he hadn't been able to do that. And now she understood his need to protect. What was it her mom always said? If you want to understand someone, take a look at their past.

"Okay," she said softly. "If Maggie would feel better hanging out with me tonight, then a slumber party it is. But she's staying in my room." She smiled a little. "We can't possibly braid each other's hair and talk about boys if she sleeps on my deck."

The tenderness in his dark eyes brought back that billowing feeling in Rachel's chest. "Good," he murmured, returning her smile. "Good. Now I won't worry about her while I'm gone."

Rachel closed her Bible, then lay back and turned off the light, a contemplative mood settling over her. She'd read passages from Revelations, then moved on to the Book of Psalms, and one verse kept repeating itself in her mind, probably because of Carrie Campbell's death. Psalm 34:18. *"The Lord is close to the brokenhearted; He rescues those who are crushed in spirit."*

For the second time today, Rachel wondered how Jake had dealt with his twin's passing. She'd needed her faith, needed her trust in God when David died. The comfort she'd received from her family and friends had been invaluable as she'd found her way back to a life without him. But without her faith, and the solid belief that David was whole and happy again, she knew she would still be broken and adrift. She hoped that sixteen-year-old Jake had turned to God, as she did, and found peace. He'd never mentioned his beliefs, but she knew he didn't go to church.

Rachel repositioned her feet, smiling when they bumped into a big, muscular lump. After a few sad, high-pitched whines when Jake left without her, Maggie had accepted Rachel's hospitality and settled in for the night. Now, as she lay curled up at the foot of the bed, she snuffled from time to time, doggie-dreaming.

"I guess I should get some sleep, too, Lord," Rachel whispered in the silence. She'd already told Him how much she regretted the vandalism done on her land. Now it was time to center on the good in her life. "Thank You for this day, and for my friends and family. Please watch over my dad as he continues to get stronger after the stroke, and keep my mom well in Your care." She paused. "Also, a friend of mine is on the road tonight. He's a good man, Lord. Keep him safe."

Then she rolled onto her side and, minutes later, welcomed the dozy, groggy beginnings of sleep…fuzzy shapes and images coalescing behind her closed eyelids.

Two hours later, a sharp bark shattered Rachel's dreams and she bolted upright to see Maggie vault from the bed and disappear into the hall. Rachel pulled on her robe and hurried to the kitchen where the Irish setter was barking and leaping against the patio's glass doors. Nerves buzzing, she snapped on the kitchen and deck lights.

Did dogs go ballistic over minor sounds in the night? Or had her intruder returned to wreak more havoc on Tim Decker's already-damaged bulldozer? Rachel snagged the dog's leash from a hook in the broom closet, then clipped it to Maggie's collar, grabbed a flashlight and pulled open the door. She couldn't let Maggie out on her own. She couldn't risk the dog being hurt when she was in her—

Maggie lunged onto the deck, yanking the leash out of her hand.

"Maggie!" Rachel rushed barefooted down the steps after her. "Maggie, get back here!"

She clicked on her flashlight, played it around until it landed on fifty pounds of reddish-gold fur. The dog stood rigidly, a low growl vibrating in her throat, her attention pinned to the construction site. Rachel looked around apprehensively, then quickly picked her way over the dirt and stones in her driveway and grabbed the leash—tugged the dog back.

Suddenly something shifted in the shadows. Rachel's fear skyrocketed—until she saw five massive figures wandering in the moonlight near the small cluster of gnarled apple trees close to the site.

She blew out a breath. "Really, Maggie. All this over a few elk?" Her yard was a constant stopover for animals making their way from the woods west of her house to the clover and trefoil across the highway. She loved to see them come through. They were shedding their winter coats now, and the bulls had just begun to sprout velvety antlers. Soon, they'd be stately and majestic again. But obviously Maggie wasn't as impressed with them as Rachel was.

"Come on," she grumbled. She gave the leash another tug, then gingerly crossed the stones and climbed the steps behind the now-unconcerned dog. "Back to bed with you. You have the luxury of staying up all night and sleeping all day. I don't."

At least this little foray took care of a question she'd been pondering. No way was she getting a dog of her own. Chronic insomnia was bad enough without having a four-legged nutcase sound the alarm every time a few elk showed up. Nope, no dogs or guns for her.

Sweat flowed from his pores as he scrambled frantically on the ground, trying to be quiet, feeling one-handed for the keys he'd dropped in the ferns and undergrowth. In the other hand, he gripped the handle of the pick and prayed he wouldn't have to use it. Where had that dog come from? She didn't have a dog!

He touched something cold and mushy in the vegetation—a disgusting slug!—but he kept his hand moving, moving. Then his fingertips bumped his key ring and his heart nearly burst in relief as he snatched it up. Fifty yards away, lights on the elevated side deck still blazed. The inside lights, too.

Jamming his keys deeply into his jeans pocket, he retrieved the pick, shovel and bag beside him and waited for the house lights to go out. He'd stopped the construction temporarily, but the problem remained. So did he stay or leave? This time, she'd blamed his nosing around on the mutt's interest in the elk. But if he alerted the dog again, she could call the police, and that could start a more diligent investigation. Bile rose in his throat, and he swallowed. Swallowed again. Maybe...maybe he was out of options.

The house went dark.

Then slowly, painstakingly, he picked his way through the woods to the logging road where he'd concealed his SUV…trembling as an anxious little voice hissed at him, whispered things he doubted he was capable of…murmured that desperate times called for desperate measures. He resisted at first. But in the end, he knew what he had to do. There was only one way to ensure his freedom, and that was to make sure the land stayed as it was. Natural, unspoiled, covered by grass and weeds.

She wouldn't need a mini golf course if she was dead.

The next morning, Rachel smiled as Maggie nosed her dog food dish aside and padded over to the stove where Rachel was frying scrambled eggs.

"I don't blame you," she said, stirring another egg to the pan. "No slumber party I ever went to ended with Kibbles 'n Bits." She gestured with her spatula. "Not that you deserve anything better after waking me up last night. But being a nice, Christian woman, I'm willing to let bygones be bygones." In a minute, she filled two plates, put Maggie's aside to cool, then set hers on the table next to her fruited yogurt and tea. She'd just asked the blessing and picked up her fork when the phone rang.

Rachel strode to the phone to check the caller ID and could tell by the number that it was a cell phone call. She picked up the receiver. "Hello?"

"So how did the slumber party go? Did she make a pest of herself or did she behave?"

The sound of his voice brought a smile to her lips and a little leap to her pulse. "We had a very nice evening. Your girl was a perfect lady. Although I have to tell you, she's not much of a conversationalist, and she really doesn't like the local wapiti."

"She barked at the elk?"

"She did, and she wasn't shy about it. They couldn't have cared less, though. They just went about their business."

"That's surprising," he returned. "She's flighty sometimes, but she usually ignores the elk."

"Maybe she didn't appreciate their being so close to the house." Rachel laughed. "Or maybe she's just on edge because of the P-R-O-W-L-E-R. Anyway, she was great company. We were just about to have breakfast."

"Then I won't keep you," he said, and her spirits fell. "I'll pick Maggie up around five or six, depending on construction traffic. It's a real mess down here."

Rachel smiled against the receiver. "Okay. See you then. Travel safely."

"Yep, see you."

She'd just settled at the table again when two honks and the sound of an approaching vehicle drew a sharp bark from Maggie. Rachel sighed. Obviously, God thought she liked cold eggs.

"Sorry, girl," she said, heading outside with Maggie trailing. "It's not him. He can't be in two places at once."

A shiny black truck with a gun rack in the back window rolled down the drive and came to a stop. Tammy Reston got out, carrying a hefty package. Tammy was a pretty blonde with the long, teased and sprayed hair of a country singer, dancer's legs and—according to the bumper sticker on her truck—a proud member of the NRA. Her camouflage skirt, tank top and cropped vest seemed to bear that out. Tammy ran

Charity's sporting goods store, had a sideline parcel delivery business and sold more blue-ribbon pies out of her backroom kitchen than the bakery did.

Rachel descended the steps to meet her.

"Hey, Rachel," Tammy said. "Got a package for you."

"Thanks. It's probably my new microwave for the store. But you didn't have to deliver it." Usually Tammy sent a postcard letting her know a package had arrived. "I could have picked it up when I went to town for my mail."

"Nah. I have a package for your gorgeous neighbor down the road, too, so I was going to be in the area anyway." She spotted Maggie then, and added wryly, "But he's not at home is he?"

Rachel hid a smile. That certainly answered her question about special deliveries. "He had a meeting."

"Probably just as well," Tammy replied, laughing. "It's hard to go home to meat loaf when you've had a peek at ambrosia."

This time Rachel did smile. "Now, now. Your Joe's a nice-looking guy."

"But he's not Jake, is he?" She looked away and got quiet for a moment, then turned back to Rachel. "I think Joe's fooling around again."

Stunned that she'd share such personal information, Rachel remained silent.

"Come on," she said quietly. "You've heard the rumors. Everyone has."

A few years ago, yes, but Rachel hadn't heard anything lately. "Why do you think he's seeing someone, Tammy?"

"Because he didn't come home a couple of nights

ago. He said he went out with the guys after bowling and knew I'd be mad, so he crashed down here at our camp." She drew a breath. "Then last night, I ran into Ellie Sennett at the Quick Mart, and she mentioned that her boyfriend had subbed for Joe Sunday night. Did you see his truck down here? It's a dark gray Silverado."

Sunday night? The same night someone vandalized Tim's bulldozer? Could there be a connection? "Tammy, I'm more than a hundred yards off the highway. Unless someone drives down here, or I'm out walking the road, I rarely see anyone. Especially at night."

"You'd tell me if you had?"

She couldn't lie. She didn't involve herself in other people's business. It was tough enough to handle her own sometimes. "I don't know."

Tammy seemed to consider that, then nodded and moved toward her truck. "I checked the camp. Someone was definitely inside since I was there last. Things had been moved around. Maybe it was Joe. But I can't get past the lie he—" She shook off the rest of it, then opened the door and changed the subject. "If you want pies again this year, give me a call."

"I do," Rachel replied. "Let's go with last year's weekly numbers—same kinds. Can you deliver them on the Thursday before Memorial Day weekend? I'm not sure what the date is."

"Absolutely. I'll make a note of it." She sent Rachel an apologetic look. "And sorry. I didn't mean to bother you with my problems."

Rachel waited until Tammy was gone, then strode back inside to reheat her cold eggs and put Maggie's on the floor. Her mind spun. Was it Joe Reston she'd seen Sunday night? And should she give that information to

Chief Perris? She hadn't heard that there'd been trouble between Joe and Tim Decker...but then, she hadn't heard that Joe was wandering again either.

Something else occurred to her. What if she dragged Joe into this and he was innocent of the vandalism but guilty of something else? If he had to supply an alibi and that alibi was female, then Tammy would be hurt. Even though Tammy was an acquaintance, not a close friend, she didn't want that to happen.

The microwave beeped, and Rachel removed her plate and carried it to the table. She couldn't make this decision alone. She needed to discuss it with someone she could trust, someone who'd be discreet. She glanced at Maggie. Someone who wasn't wearing a collar and a fur coat.

Just after five o'clock, Maggie jumped up from her dozing position on the bathhouse floor and bolted for the exit, whining to be let out. A second later, the sound of a familiar truck reached Rachel's ears. She put down her paintbrush. Apparently, Jake had found the note she'd taped to the camp store telling him where they'd be.

"Okay, girl," she said, opening the door. "Go to it. I'll bet he missed you, too."

The chuckles and yelping outside went on for a half minute while Rachel replaced the paint can's lid and rinsed her brush. Then Jake came to the door, and she felt that tingle again. She liked the way his collarless knit shirt clung to his shoulders and biceps. Burgundy was definitely his color. It complemented his year-round tan.

"Hi. How did your meeting go?"

He smiled. "Like most of them. Some issues were resolved, others were tabled. Have you had dinner?"

"No, but Maggie and I were thinking about grilling hamburgers. I'm afraid she's lost that loving feeling for her dog food."

"No surprise there," he said, grinning. "She thinks she's human." He paused. "Getting back to food, how about something easier than hamburgers?"

Rachel laughed. "Like what? Cold cereal?"

"No, you kept Maggie safe from the boogeyman last night, and I want to thank you with dinner. Nothing fancy, just chicken at the diner and maybe some ice cream for dessert."

For a long, uneasy moment, Rachel stood silently, a lump in her throat. She wanted to say yes. She did. Jake was a good man, and everything about him lately seemed to make her...react. But somewhere in her mind and heart, the part of her that would always love David still ached when she considered moving on with that "other" aspect of her life.

She was saved from trying to explain when his expression darkened and he got the message.

"Then again," he said coolly, "maybe dinner in town isn't a good idea. After all, people would see us together, and they might make assumptions. The way gossip spreads around here, it would take weeks to set everyone straight." He paused. "We wouldn't want anyone to get the wrong idea."

A tidal wave of remorse hit her. "Jake, I don't want you to get the wrong idea. It's not—" How did she say this without sounding positively horrible? "It's not as though I don't want to be seen with you, if that's what you're thinking. We're friends." But while having coffee or lunch with a vital, good-looking man seemed incidental, having dinner was significant. "I haven't been to dinner with a man since—" She stopped before she said David's name and sighed.

She wasn't totally clueless. She knew something was happening between them, but she also knew that she wasn't ready yet. "Will you and Maggie stay for hamburgers and macaroni salad?" she asked gently. "I'd really like that. Besides, there's something I'd like to talk over with you."

He waited for her to go on.

"Tammy Reston came by to deliver a package this morning and said something that could be important. It might be connected to Tim's trouble."

It took Jake so long to reply that she thought he'd refuse. Finally, he nodded and said, "Sure. Maggie and I would like to stay." But the warmth in his dark eyes seemed to have dimmed at the same rate as the joy in her heart.

FOUR

Irritated with himself, Jake roared up his long gravel driveway, ground to a stop beside his log home and cut his vehicle's engine. If there was anything he hated, it was pretending to be happy. He wasn't any good at it, and it made his stomach feel like a bag of rocks. His only consolation was Rachel had done her share of pretending, too—and she wasn't any better at it than he was. He would have ducked out and headed for home a lot sooner if not for their discussion about Tammy and Joe Reston.

Snatching his duffle bag from the backseat, he climbed out of his truck, slammed the door behind him and stalked up the gravel path to his porch. He was halfway there when he realized he'd left something behind. Scowling, he retraced his steps, let Maggie out and took the path to the house again.

Why are you so wired? a nagging voice said. You knew how she felt about dating. Over the past six months, she's let you know she's still grieving in a dozen different ways. Besides, you're not looking for an involvement, right?

"That's right," Jake muttered, unlocking the door and stepping inside. "I'm not." And it wasn't a date, he grumbled silently. It was just some quick thank-you food she didn't have to cook herself. What was the big deal about that?

He dropped his duffle on a brown leather armchair that matched his sofa and looked fairly decent with the wood lamps on his tables. Then he continued into his home office to check his phone messages and see if Outdoor Club adviser Alex Liston had gotten back to him about the club's field trip Thursday. Hopefully, they'd find a few elk calves to process. Elk mothers were good at hiding their offspring.

The red light was blinking.

Jabbing the play button, Jake dropped into the swivel chair in front of his computer hutch. He had two messages. The first call was from his mother—a follow-up call after Julie's visit to her doctor.

"Hi, honey, it's official!" she sang happily. "You're going to be an uncle. Greg and Julie are due at the end of the year. Maybe we'll have a Christmas baby." There was a slight pause—unusual for her because she generally spoke rapid-fire. "Where are you? You're never home. Pick up if you're there." She waited a few seconds, then gave up. "Okay, love you. Hope you're having a good day."

Oh, yeah. He was having a peachy day.

After a beep, the second message played. "Jake, it's Alex Liston at the middle school. We'll have fifteen students for the field trip. The kids know they'll need a packed lunch, and all of the permission slips are in, so we're a go. Looking forward to seeing you Thursday morning at nine."

Well, *that* plan had worked out at least.

Jake glanced at his watch, saw that it was barely

seven-ten, then returned his mother's call and phoned his brother and sister-in-law with his congratulations. He was glad for Greg and Julie, but his happiness for them was tempered by a touch of what-might-have-been. Their mom had always been pretty good at getting what she wanted from her sons, and after a few good-natured back and forths, he and Greg had agreed to a double-wedding ceremony with both couples promising to love, honor and cherish at the same time. Obviously, only one couple had made it to the altar last November. Now he couldn't help thinking that if Heather'd had a passing interest in fidelity, they might have had a child on the way, too. Unfortunately, Heather's interests had been elsewhere.

"Come on, Maggie," he said, abruptly pushing to his feet. "Let's go fill the bird feeders." He didn't need to go over his notes for the lecture portion of the field trip. He'd given it dozens of times when he'd lived and worked in Potter County. What he needed was to concentrate on something else.

Dutifully, Maggie padded behind him to his screened-in back porch. In a corner, near a couple of weathered Adirondack chairs that had come with the house, sat a forty-pound bag of black oil sunflower seeds. Reaching inside, he used the scoop to fill a pail, then took both outside and got to work. A jittery nuthatch took off as he approached the feeders—and his traitorous dog did the same. Not that he blamed her. He wasn't the best company this evening.

He forced himself to think about Joe Reston. He knew the man slightly. Last month, Reston and a handful of concerned citizens had met with him to complain about last year's crop damage by the elk. Reston was a hothead, but as he'd told Rachel, that didn't make him a suspect unless there was bad blood between Reston and Tim Decker. And if the two men were on the outs, Reston's would have been the first name Tim offered when the chief asked if he had any enemies. He was glad when Rachel agreed he was right. After seeing the chief in action yesterday, Jake suspected that Perris would have considered any "help" from Rachel an affront to his capabilities, and would have shown her the door pronto.

He was midway through filling the feeders when his phone rang. Putting down the bucket, Jake strode back to the house and answered it on the fifth ring. He picked up just before his answering machine clicked on.

"Hi, it's me," a soft voice said after his "hello." "I can't stop thinking about tonight. Is everything okay between us?"

Us? There *was* no us. "Why wouldn't it be?" he asked.

"Because you were upset when you left. I know you tried to hide it, but we've known each other for a while now, and I can tell when something's bothering you. Do we— Do we need to talk about my turning down your dinner invitation?"

And give him the opportunity to say what he'd been thinking for the past month? I know David was a nice guy, and you loved him, but I'm tired of hearing about your late-husband every forty-five minutes. Yeah, that would be classy—especially because he had no ties on her and didn't want any. Jake drew a breath, then let it out. If pretending to be happy was number one on his hate-to-do list, uneasy conversations ran a close second. He could go toe-to-toe with any man, had no problem getting down and dirty with thugs and never flinched when he had to draw his sidearm. But Rachel was another matter.

"No, we don't need to talk. I understand why you said no."

"You're sure?"

"Yeah," he returned honestly. "I'm sorry. I was lousy company tonight."

"It's okay. You had a long day."

Yes, he had, but that wasn't why he'd been distant. And it wasn't okay. "Look," he said quietly, "on Thursday, a wildlife biologist, wildlife vet and I are taking a bunch of sixth graders out in the field, hopefully to collar and tag a couple of elk calves. I think I told you about the four-year mortality study the game commission's doing."

"Yes, you mentioned it."

"Would you like to join us? I know you have a lot to do before your opening, but if you can get away for a couple of hours, I think you'd enjoy it."

The relief in her voice was nearly palpable, and once again, he felt like a jerk for making her worry.

"I'd like that. What time and where should I meet you?"

The sun was still trying to burn off the morning fog Thursday as Rachel stood with biologist Tom Keene and veterinarian Chaz Haskell, watching Jake line up fifteen smiling, excited sixth graders at the top of a grassy field. Alex Liston and another teacher took their places at the opposite end of the long horizontal line.

"Okay," Jake instructed. "We're all going to walk slowly, quietly and carefully down through the high grass—all the way to the road. While their mothers are away, newborns lie flat on the ground in 'hider position' so they don't reveal their presence to a potential predator. Sometimes they don't even blink an eye. If you spot one, say, 'Calf on the ground.' Then we'll all circle the calf to discourage it from running, and Dr. Haskell, Mr. Keene and I will take over. Any questions?"

A ponytailed girl raised her hand. "Can we touch the calves?"

"Sorry, but no. We don't want to traumatize them any more than we have to."

"We can take pictures, though, right?" a freckle-faced kid in a baseball cap asked.

"Sure, that's what you're here for. To learn and have fun. But wait until I give the word."

To Rachel's delight, it didn't take long for the first calf to be located—all splayed out and stone-still against the ground. They walked toward it. Suddenly, it scrambled to its feet—tried to run. At a quick sprint, Jake restrained it, then eased it back on the ground. He gave the word, and a dozen cameras came out of pockets and fanny packs.

He was a cutie, Rachel decided, liking the gentle way Jake and his crew covered its eyes, then laid the spotted, copper-colored calf on a net and hooked the net to a suspension scale to be weighed. Jake lifted the calf off the ground. Amazingly, the little guy remained relatively calm.

"Forty-two pounds," Haskell said.

"Pretty big baby, isn't it?" Jake said to the elated kids. "And he's only a few days old."

He sent Rachel a private smile, and she smiled back. Like wild horses out west, the massive elk and their offspring were natural treasures, and brought a vital majesty to the county forests...just as the tall man sharing this moment with her brought something vital to Rachel.

Jake turned the calf over to the vet and biologist, then moved to Rachel's side. He addressed the teachers and kids again while Haskell and Keene examined the calf, and fitted him with an ear tag and a yellow radio collar. "Every collar transmits a different signal to the game commission's telemetry equipment. Now we'll be able to pinpoint his location and check him periodically—make sure he's healthy and doing well. Questions?"

A hand went up. "He's going to get big. Won't he choke if the collar gets too tight?"

Jake smiled. "He'll be fine. The collar's expandable. The stitching will break away as he grows."

After the kids had snapped a few more photos and named their calf, Rachel smiled along with the others as "Jimmy" ran up the hill where his nervous mother stood watching.

Jake spoke quietly to Rachel. "Glad you came?" He wore his tan uniform today.

"Very," she replied, glad to be talking again without that clenching uneasiness. She hadn't realized how important his friendship was to her until he'd left the night before last and she'd felt an acute sense of loss. It had still taken her a half hour to gather enough courage to call him. "I have to say that Jimmy was a lot cuter before he was fitted with the ear tag and collar, though."

"True. Unfortunately, that's the way it has to be." He nodded toward the kids and professionals who were gearing up to walk the next field. "Ready to try again?"

"Absolutely," Rachel replied with a smile. And she wasn't referring to spotting newborn calves.

Late that afternoon, after Haskell, Keene and the teachers and students had gone, Rachel watched Jake toss the suspension scale into the back of his truck, then return to where she stood beside her red Explorer. She liked the way he moved. Unhurried, yet with purpose. A light breeze tempered the afternoon heat and tossed his dark brown hair.

"Three calves," he said. "Not bad for this early in the birthing season. Nice of the weatherman to give us a good day. We should thank him."

"Wrong. The weatherman didn't supply the blue skies and sunshine." She pointed skyward. "He did."

For a second, Jake seemed at a loss for words. Then he grinned and tapped her sunburned nose. "Planning to thank Him for your sunburn, too? You're going to look like Rudolph after the sun sets."

"I thank Him for everything." She paused. "But I get the feeling you don't."

Jake leaned a hip against the red SUV's front fender. "I'm just not...churchy."

"Were you ever?"

He thought about that. "Yeah, I guess so. I was raised a Christian. My dad's an agnostic, but my mom made sure Carrie, Greg and I attended services. Things changed for me after my sister was killed, though."

"You blamed God."

"You bet. I couldn't believe He'd allow something like that to happen to her. Then, when I was through being mad…I guess I just stopped caring. Faith wasn't high on my priority list then anyway. I was sixteen and into friends, girls and every sport you can name." He shrugged. "After that, the distractions of daily living pretty much pushed religion to the background. People get busy, Rachel."

She didn't understand that. She'd never be too busy for God. She needed the peace that came with being a woman of faith. "No problem," she returned smiling. "He'll be there for you the next time you need Him." She hesitated for a moment, then her nosy self asked the question. "So…the next time you planned to be in a church was on your wedding day?"

He raised a dark eyebrow, but he still replied, "That was the plan."

"Can I ask why it didn't work out?"

He smiled. "You can ask, but it's not something I feel comfortable talking about with you, so you won't be getting an answer. Let's just say that I'm now one of those confirmed bachelors you've heard about."

The smart thing to do was to back off. But after the hurt—or anger—she'd heard in his voice a few days ago, she knew he was still coming to terms with whatever had happened. "Would you feel better discussing it with someone else?"

Jake straightened from the car and met her eyes, though not in an adversarial way. "Why do you think I need to talk to anyone?"

"So you can move on and be happy."

"I have moved on. I am happy. But you know what would make me even happier?"

She waited expectantly. "What?"

"Helping you paint the bathhouses a little later. This

field trip cost you a whole day's work, and I'm feeling guilty about it. I need to make it up to you."

Rachel sighed. Once again, he was tabling the discussion. *And that's his prerogative,* a small voice reminded her. "This trip didn't cost me anything. I had fun, and I loved being up close and personal with the elk calves. As for the bathhouses…thanks for offering, but I finished them yesterday."

"I see. Then you're totally ready to open Memorial Day weekend."

She rolled her eyes. "I wish." There was still an enormous amount of work to do.

"That's what I thought. I saw a case of cedar stain near a stack of cartons when I was in your store the other day. I assume the stain's for the picnic tables at the campsites."

"It is. The tables get a fresh coat every season. It's time consuming, but it's a lot cheaper than replacing them."

"Then I'll see you after I write my report and take care of a couple of things. Okay?"

With all the work ahead of her, and her summer help not showing up for two weeks, it would be lunacy to refuse. But since Tuesday night, she'd felt as though she were walking an emotional tightrope. Worse, she didn't know if the tension was her own doing or his. She glanced at her wristwatch: twelve-forty. "You're sure you don't have work of your own to do?"

"I'm sure."

"Okay, then I accept." She opened her car door. "I have to run a few errands in town and pick up some things for the store. But I should be back by four."

"Great. I'll see you then."

Rachel watched him walk to the green truck with the PA Game Commission logo on the side, unable to look away from his broad shoulders and loose, confident gait. Then she slipped inside her Explorer, started the engine and drove off, wishing she could see inside his head. Wishing he'd tell her what he was thinking and feeling. Jake Campbell was the most guarded man she'd ever known.

He was also the most intriguing.

"I'm so glad you're back," Rachel said an hour later as she followed Jenna Harper outside to the B & B's wide wraparound porch. She'd missed her sounding board and best friend. "Did you have fun?"

"I did," Jenna replied with a smile. "It was great to spend time with my mom, but she's a busy bee, and any more than a week with me would've had her climbing the walls. She's used to being out and about."

"Which you can't do."

Jenna sent her an uneasy look. "Not in Michigan."

Not here in Charity either. Most people had something in their past they wish they could change—baggage they couldn't unload. But her beautiful friend's was as bad as it got without costing a life.

Jenna set a tray holding frosted glasses of lemonade and a small basket of tiny orange muffins on the glass-topped white-wicker table, then crossed to the porch's edge to lower a sun-shading white vinyl blind. "But even if I'd felt comfortable running to the malls or whatever with my mom, I had to get back." She joined Rachel on the wicker sofa. "With tourist season on the way, it's going to get busy around here. But I'm not telling you anything you don't know."

"Around here" was Jenna's Blackberry Hill Bed and Breakfast, a lovely pink-and-white Victorian inn with loads of white gingerbread surrounded by rhododendrons and azaleas that were just beginning to bloom. Although she, Jenna and Margo McBride Blackburn had been best friends all through high school, they'd lost touch after Jenna and her mother moved to Michigan. Jenna had returned to Charity a little over two years ago to buy and manage her great-aunt Molly Jennings's B & B, but it wasn't by choice. She didn't talk about the jealous ex-suitor who'd stabbed her. But Jenna believed he was still out there somewhere, eluding the police and waiting for an opportunity to finish what he'd started. Jenna was running.

"I imagine reservations are pouring into the campground, too. Are you ready?"

Rachel took a sip of lemonade. "I'm getting there. I have vendors to call, supplies to shelve and some staining to do—and the game room could use a coat of paint. But I'll get it done." She frowned. "Doesn't look like my putt-putt course will open anytime soon, though."

Jenna nodded. "So I've heard. I stopped at the hardware store when I got back yesterday, and Ben mentioned Tim Decker's troubles. He seemed to think I had the inside track because we're friends. Do the police have any leads?"

"Not according to Tim. I saw him a few minutes ago. He said the bearings are shot in his machine—whatever that means. But his second dozer should be free in a week, so he hopes to get back to my project then."

Jenna offered the muffins to Rachel, but she thanked her and declined. She took another sip of her lemonade, then felt a silly flutter in her stomach as she began hesitantly. "You remember my neighbor Jake Campbell, don't you?"

"Sure. Nice guy." Jenna's blue eyes danced beneath her side-swept dark blond bangs as she amended her description. "Nice, tall, good-looking, muscular guy. Or am I thinking of someone else?"

Feeling her cheeks warm, Rachel said, "No, I think we're talking about the same man."

"Okay. What about him? Is something going on?"

"I don't know," she returned quietly. "Maybe. It's just so hard to get past..."

Jenna nodded her understanding. "David."

Rachel felt her throat tighten. "I still miss him, Jen. I can't imagine ever not missing him."

"I know. The two of you were good together. But now there's Jake."

"Yes."

"And you feel guilty."

Rachel nodded. "I like him. He makes me feel good just being around him. He's fun and he's smart...and caring about him feels so wrong and so right at the same time."

Jenna squeezed Rachel's hand and she squeezed back, relieved to finally be talking about her feelings for him.

"Can I say something without making you cry?" Jenna asked.

"Probably not," Rachel returned, laughing a little and already seeing her friend through watery eyes. "But go ahead."

Jenna spoke softly. "Anyone who knew you and David could see the love you had for each other. But, honey, he can't come back to you. That's not the way life works." Jenna sent her a sad smile as tears spilled over Rachel's cheeks. "A love that big isn't selfish. David adored you. He'd want you to be happy, wouldn't he?"

Drawing a trembling breath, Rachel nodded. But knowing that and acting on that knowledge were two very different things.

Later, wrapped in the variegated blue afghan her grandmother had crocheted, Rachel sat on her deck, curled in a redwood lounge chair, staring through a break in the trees above her driveway. Overhead in the inky blackness, a plane on a night flight blinked red and green, momentarily distracting her from God's magnificent light show. She'd doused all the lights in her home except for the forty-watt bulb glowing in her over-the-range microwave, and the stars seemed to shimmer and gleam in stereo. It was a perfect night for soul searching…a perfect night to consider questions that had caromed around in her mind since her visit with Jenna.

"What do I do about this, God?' she murmured. "I loved David with all my heart. You know that. But Jenna's right. He wouldn't want me to give up a chance at happiness. That's the kind of man he was, and it's what I would have wanted for him if our lives—our deaths—had been reversed." She watched the plane disappear behind the trees—searched for God in the stars. "As for Jake… You saw him tonight, staining my picnic tables, then leaving and bringing back pizza. But I don't know if he's being a good neighbor, if he's still in protective mode, or something else. And is this the right time for 'something else'?"

Fireflies flitted in the air, their tiny beacons flashing in the darkness—but throwing no light at all on her conflicted thoughts. She shifted on the lounger, pulled her bare feet up under the afghan. "His broken engagement soured him on marriage, so he's not looking for anything permanent. I get that." But what happened if she began to care about Jake too deeply? Even though her own lack of decisiveness still had her emotionally shackled, she wasn't sure how she felt about a surface relationship with him. What if she would always be someone he could enjoy chicken and ice cream with, believing she'd never want or expect anything more?

A loud bang and crash came from under her deck. Jumping up, Rachel waved a hand to turn on her motion lights and rushed down the steps in time to see—as she expected—two bristly lumps hurry away from her trash cans. Raccoons. You'd think they'd realize that when the trash cans were outside, they were empty. The best defense against marauding animals was to keep refuse inside until the morning that it was collected—which had happened today. But she'd failed to return the cans to her mud room.

So much for a night of soul searching.

Moving inside, then descending her basement steps, she unlocked the ground-level door, lugged the trash cans back inside and locked up again. Maybe all that noise was her cue to get some sleep. Jake wasn't the only one who'd had a long, tiring day. She was slowly finding out that emotional stress could be just as draining.

A few hours later, she was thoroughly annoyed to realize she was coming awake again and tried to fight it. She burrowed deeper into her pillow, tried to concentrate on the dream she'd left behind. It was a good one. She and Jenna were crocheting baby booties, but she didn't know who they were for. She drew a breath—coughed. Coughed again. She would go back to sleep. She couldn't keep—

Rachel bolted upright in bed, alarm bells clanging in her head. She flew to her bedroom window and saw flames licking upward over the siding.

Dear God! Her house was on fire!

FIVE

Terrified, Rachel ran to her nightstand, grabbed her cordless handset and raced for the living room. Suddenly, her smoke and heat detectors began to beep and scream. She punched in 9-1-1—jerked the phone to her ear. No dial tone! Her panic escalated. Rushing to her kitchen phone, she yanked the receiver off the hook and released another frightened breath. Still no dial tone!

Her thoughts ran wild. Save what you can! No! Get out, get out! Then: the camp store has a phone! The smoke was faint, and the fire was at the rear corner of the house. She had time. Rachel was through the patio door in seconds and bolting down the steps. She hit the driveway's limestone chips at a run. Behind her, motion lights clicked on.

She still had lights! Thank you, Jesus! Now please, please let the phone work!

Eighty yards away, the camp store's faint overnight lighting showed the way. She ran faster, barely aware of the stones cutting into her feet. Sixty yards. Forty. Twenty. Gasping, she leaped onto the stoop, tried the door. Locked! She yanked the wooden No Pets Inside, Please sign off the siding beside the door and smashed the glass pane—fumbled an arm inside to free the latch.

Seconds later she uttered a shaky prayer of thanks again.

She had a dial tone!

Every nerve in his body pulsed and thumped as Jake yanked a T-shirt over his jeans, jammed his feet into his boots and strode for the door. He jerked his jacket from the back of a kitchen chair on his way out. The police scanner beside his bed was still squawking orders to and from firemen and emergency personnel on their way to the campground.

Maggie ran after him through his still-open door—jumped into the truck with him when he slid behind the wheel. Then he gunned the engine and roared out of his driveway, his brain all needles and fear. Rachel was too vigilant to have accidentally caused the fire, and she was a stickler for upkeep. No old paint cans or turpentine rags would be lying around waiting to spontaneously combust. That pile of rocks was back in his belly. He wasn't an alarmist by nature, and he really didn't like where his thoughts were headed. But after seeing a man skulking around her place on Sunday night, what were the odds that Rachel's fire was a coincidence? A small voice answered, *Low, but keep an open mind.*

Jake rounded the deep curve in the road, saw the sign for her campground in his headlights, then touched a boot to the brake to make the turn. He flew over the uneven lane and skidded to a stop outside her store. She'd told the dispatcher that's where she was calling from. Already, the smell of smoke permeated the truck's cab.

Jake ordered Maggie to stay, then leaped out and quickly ascended the stoop. There was broken glass all over—and no sign of Rachel. He ran down the driveway. He could see flames now, could see smoke billowing from the far side of the house. Jake's stomach fell to his feet when he spotted her on the deck. She threw an armful of clothes, books and a heavy case over the railing, most of it landing beside her red Explorer with the campground emblem on its side.

He accelerated, shouted at the top of his lungs. "Rachel! Get out of there!"

"I'll be right back!" she cried.

"No! Get out of there now!" he repeated. "There's nothing in your house worth dying for!" But she'd already covered her nose and mouth with a cloth and was rushing back inside.

Jake took the stairs two at a time, his heart pounding triple time. "Rachel!"

She reappeared, clutching something tightly against her chest.

Latching on to her wrist, he tugged her down the stairs. The blaze had found its voice now, angry orange flames roaring as they lit the night, devouring siding and igniting roof shingles.

She pulled away—rushed to the items scattered on the ground. "Help me grab my things! Throw them in my car!"

Arguing was useless, so he moved swiftly, then hustled her into the passenger seat and jumped behind the wheel. The keys were in the ignition. Hitting the gas, he backed all the way up the drive, then swerved into a parking space outside the camp store.

He shot her a look of total disbelief, worry making his tone harsher than he intended. "For the love of God, Rachel, what were you thinking, running into a burning house? You have a propane tank out back that could blow to kingdom come and take you with it. What was so important that you'd risk—"

She jerked a look at him. "Don't yell at me!" Then her face crumbled, and she started to cry. Slowly, she turned the wedding photo she'd held to her chest to face him, and her voice dropped to a sad, teary whisper. "I couldn't just leave him in there."

Her words hit him squarely in the heart. He couldn't have felt lower if he'd attacked her physically. Sighing, Jake slid over on the seat and reached for her...wrapped her in his arms as tightly as David Patterson's picture would permit.

"I'm so sorry," he murmured. "I know you couldn't." But as much as he wanted to keep holding her, with every tick of the clock, the fire crept closer to that propane tank. Easing her away, he spoke softly but seriously. "Rachel, it's the middle of the night. It'll take the firemen time to get here. We should try to slow down the fire—keep the propane tank cool."

Jake saw her eyes widen as she realized how much worse the situation could become. The woods, her cabins and store—her very livelihood—could go up in a fireball explosion that seared the sky.

"Your garden hose has a high pressure nozzle," he said quickly, opening the car door. "It'll spray a hundred feet." Whether that would do any good was a mystery, but they had to try.

He didn't have to say another word. She was already halfway out of the car.

Hours later, Rachel stood by Jake's side, tears streaming again as she watched volunteer firemen training their hoses on hot spots, and continuing to wet the utility shed where David's truck, golf cart and lawnmowers were stored—wet down the trees surrounding her home. Utility servicemen still milled around, talking to firemen and drinking coffee supplied by the ladies of the firemen's auxiliary.

The house itself was all but gone now, nothing left but charred timbers, a creek stone chimney that wouldn't give up, and the acrid smell of burned memories she would remember all of her life. It hurt so much that she didn't trust herself to speak.

Jake slid his arm around her shoulders, and she turned into him, holding on tightly and grateful for his strength.

"Let's go back to the camp store," he murmured against her temple. "We can grab another cup of coffee or a donut or just sit for a while." After the firemen had arrived, Jake had pulled a pair of flip-flops, bottled water, towels and antiseptic spray from her store shelves. Then, over her teary objections, he'd knelt down to clean the dirt from her feet and attend a bloody cut she didn't know she had. "You should give your foot a rest. There's nothing you can do here."

She knew that, but somehow she couldn't stop watching, couldn't stop monitoring every word the firemen and hazmat team called to each other. She'd managed to save some of her things; besides her wedding portrait, she'd gathered a photo album, the clothes from her dryer and her security box. Thankfully, David had insisted the box be placed in the laundry room off the kitchen—not in the bedroom or living room where thieves might expect it to be.

Rachel swallowed hard. Electric service to her home

had been separate from the store and campsites, and light poles throughout the campground glowed in the lingering smoke and haze. She stepped back from him, but not very far. "You're a good man."

"I try," he said quietly.

"You do more than try." He'd barely left her side since he'd arrived except for a few minutes a half hour ago. Once it was certain that the fire wouldn't spread to the woods, he'd driven Maggie back home and put her in her pen. "I'll never be able to thank you enough for everything you've done tonight."

He smiled. "Well, it's not as if I was busy doing anything else." At some point, he'd slipped his green jacket over her dorm shirt—startling her because she'd forgotten how she was dressed. Now he adjusted it on her shoulders. "Come on. The firemen's auxiliary's been working hard back at the store. You don't want the ladies to think they're unappreciated, do you?"

"No," she said. "I wouldn't want that."

They were preparing to walk back up the lane to the store when, from some distance away, Fire Chief Ben Caruthers called for Rachel to wait.

"Give me a minute?" she said to Jake, automatically backing up several feet.

"Sure."

"I'll catch up with you as soon as I'm through."

Dressed in smoke-smudged, dull-gold bunker pants and an insulated coat striped with reflective tape, Ben came toward her. An SCBA mask dangled from his neck. Like many of the firemen who attended her church—Roy Blair, Nate, Joe Reston and the Atkins brothers—Ben had offered his sympathies earlier. She wasn't surprised when Reverend and Mrs. Landers showed up to offer their prayers and visit for a few minutes. They were loving, caring people who did whatever needed to be done for St. John's congregation, day or night. The big surprise was the courtesy that off-duty Chief of Police Lon Perris had shown her. Maybe it was the lack of a uniform and a gun on his hip that seemed to soften his demeanor. But by the time Charity P.D. officers Charlie Banks and newly hired Caleb "Call" Drago took him aside to talk, she was nearly ready to change her opinion of him.

Ben pulled off his helmet and heavy gloves as he reached her—kept his insulated hood on. "Sorry, Rachel. The house was just too far gone by the time we got here. But you were insured and you can rebuild. Focus on that—and the fact that you got out alive."

"I am, Ben. And believe me, I'm grateful." But she couldn't think about rebuilding right now. She was too worried that she might have inadvertently caused the fire. "Do you know how it started? I can't think of anything I did that might have—"

Caruthers glanced aside for an uneasy moment, then said, "I can't say, Rachel. That's up to the fire marshal to determine. I expect he'll be here tomorrow." He exhaled heavily. "In the meantime, what are your plans? Do you know where you'll be staying? We'll need to get in touch with you."

A firm voice came from behind her. "She'll be staying with me."

Rachel turned sharply and her eyes welled with tears again. "Jenna."

"I'm so sorry," Jenna murmured, hugging Rachel close. "I'm so, so sorry."

Rachel tried to keep her voice from cracking but

failed. It was nearly daybreak, and Jenna should have been in her kitchen preparing breakfast pastries for her guests. "Jen, you shouldn't be here."

"Of course I should. You're my friend."

"You have an inn to run."

"Not for another three days. I'm not reopening until Monday."

Rachel sighed. That was right. They'd talked about it yesterday. Or was it the day before? She couldn't think. Everything except the present was a blur. "How did you know about the fire?"

With a cheerless smile, Jenna turned her to face Jake, and there was no need for her friend to answer. "You've been a busy boy tonight," she murmured.

He ambled closer. "I figured you'd eventually get sick of me, and want someone who could actually do you some good. I phoned Jenna when I took Maggie back home."

"But how did you—?"

"—know to call Jenna?" He smiled. "You've mentioned her enough times that I knew she was important to you. Not all men have selective hearing."

Gratitude cinched her voice. "I owe you."

He shook his head. "Anyone who knows you would have done the same." He glanced around, seemed satisfied that she was in good hands, then backed away. "I'll see you later. If you need anything, holler." He turned to Jenna. "You have my phone number. Thanks for coming."

"Thanks for calling," she replied. "I just wish you'd done it sooner."

Then Rachel watched as he strode back to the camp

store where his truck waited and—not for the first time tonight—thanked God for his friendship.

Why wasn't she *dead?* Why wasn't this *over?*

He was far from the madness of smoke and flames now, but his heart still pounded so frantically that he feared he'd stroke out. Rushing to the bathroom medicine chest, he snatched a bottle of aspirin from the shelf and turned on the cold water spigot. Pills clacked against plastic as he shook out two tablets, then swallowed them with a handful of water. He jammed the bottle back inside the mirrored chest and stared at his reflection.

He could still feel the heat of the fire, still feel the weight of his gear and the SCBA mask pressing into his face. And despite his shower, he could still smell the stench of smoke.

He wet his hands—pumped liquid soap into his palm and scrubbed his face. Pushed frothy bubbles into his nostrils to cover the smell.

He'd been smart about the fire—used a common accelerant that would positively point to arson and rule out an educated fireman. In this day and age of forensics, it was nearly impossible to create an "accidental" fire. Kerosene and gasoline would have done the trick because they had low flash points. But ultimately he'd chosen one that fit his purposes better in the event that Rachel lived through the blaze. He'd used the same stove-and-lantern fuel she sold in her store, and in doing that, planted a little seed that she might have started the blaze herself.

He walked around, fretted, wondered if the aspirin was burning a hole in his stomach lining. He'd heard of repressed—or was that suppressed?—memories. What if she woke up one morning and realized he was the man she'd seen Sunday night? Tears formed in his eyes. She'd tell. And life as he knew it would be over. Everything he'd worked for would be over!

Suddenly his insides revolted, and with an anguished cry, he bent over the toilet and emptied his stomach. "God, help me," he whispered gripping the bowl. But he doubted that God was listening anymore.

Rachel swam toward consciousness in the shaded room, the world around her slowly taking shape. Two tall posters rose at the bottom of her cozy bed, and from somewhere to her left, a soft breeze touched her face. She smiled—stretched a little.

Then reality swept away contentment, and a cold hard stone settled on her heart. She was at Jenna's, in one of her rooms at the Blackberry. Her home and everything in it was gone.

It all came back to her. She remembered the fire, remembered the fear...remembered Jake holding her and washing her feet.

"Come on. Sit down and let me do this. Looks like you stepped on a piece of glass—probably when you broke into the store."

"I'm okay. I can do it."

"I know you can," he'd replied, the compassion in his eyes touching her. *"But let me."*

She smiled sadly. Who would have thought a big man could be so gentle?

Blinking back tears, she got out of bed, grimaced a little when her left foot touched the floor, then pulled Jenna's robe over the nightgown she'd borrowed. She'd asked Jenna to wake her if she slept past twelve-thirty, and according to the clock beside the bed, it was nearly that now. She found her friend in the sunny little breakfast nook off the kitchen, setting the table with white china cups, saucers and plates ringed in tiny pink roses. It was a lovely, welcome sight after the horror of charred wood and broken dreams.

"Good afternoon," Jenna said, smiling and looking up. "Did you sleep well?"

"Better than I can remember," Rachel replied, returning her smile. She took a seat. "If all the beds in the Blackberry are as comfortable as mine, no wonder business is booming."

"I'm not sure it's booming," Jenna said, pouring coffee for the two of them. "But reservations are coming in. I'll be full—except for your room—on Monday."

"How wonderful," Rachel returned, then took in the table. Glazed cranberry-almond scones were piled on a footed crystal platter, and at each of their place settings, glasses of orange juice sat beside small bowls of chilled berries and fruit. Pale green rings held pink linen napkins.

She wasn't used to such lavishness. She loved nice things and enjoyed dressing up for special occasions. But for the most part, she was a hot dogs-and-mountains, pies-over-a-fire woman. It still felt wonderful to be pampered—if only for a day or two.

Jenna was moving again, taking a bowl of whipped cream from the refrigerator, then adding a huge dollop of it to their fruit. "Now what else can I get you? An omelet? Cereal? Waffles?"

Rachel had to laugh. "Nothing. This is almost more than I can handle."

"You're sure? It wouldn't be any trouble."

"I'm sure."

"Okay, then." She took a seat across from Rachel and drew a deep breath. "What's your plan today?"

The hurt came back. "I guess I should contact my insurance company first. Then I'll call Ben. He said the fire marshal would probably be investigating today. And I suppose I should drive down to the campground—see what I have to work with in the light of day."

Jenna's look softened. "That should be a lot of fun. Need some company? I'm not busy today."

"Thanks, but I need to face this on my own. Besides, I'll be there for a while. I need to have the glass replaced in my door, and call my guests—give them the option of bowing out. I'm afraid the smell of the fire could linger for a while."

"What about your parents?"

"I know I should call them—at least let my mom know. But with Dad still recovering… Jenna, I just can't. She'd want to be with both of us, and it would tear her apart."

Jenna stirred cream and sugar into her coffee. "They lived here for a lot of years. What if they hear it from someone they still keep in touch with? This *is* the era of texting, emails and instant messaging."

Rachel sighed. "I guess I'll deal with that if it happens."

Her dad's job had taken her parents back to historic Williamsburg following her wedding, and Rachel's Southern belle mom had loved returning to her roots on the James River where so much history had been made. Then two months ago, her dad had suffered a slight stroke, and Rachel had hurried to Virginia. Toward the end of her two-week visit, she'd convinced her mom to surrender her dad's care to her aunt Chelsea for a few hours, and they'd toured an old plantation. Her mom had insisted that she'd had fun, soaking up tales of traveling tinkers and spoon-stealing union officers. But Rachel knew she'd worried constantly. The last thing she wanted to do was add to her worries.

Reluctantly, she met Jenna's eyes. They were the same lovely blue as the figure-skimming V-neck rib-knit top she wore with matching slacks and a tiny pearl timepiece dangling from long, thin chains. Rachel couldn't recall a night or day when her friend didn't look as if she'd stepped out of a fashion magazine. "I have a favor to ask."

"Anything. If I have it, it's yours."

"I need to borrow something to wear so I can shop for my own. I think the only clothes I salvaged are sweats."

Jenna smiled. "My closet is your closet." Then she asked the blessing, and Rachel added to it.

"Thank you for giving me good friends and neighbors, Lord. Bless them, especially Jenna who's given me a home, the firemen who worked so tirelessly…and my friend Jake who always seems to know exactly what to say and do." She smiled at Jenna. "Amen. Now pass those wonderful scones. I'm starving."

At four-fifteen, Jake pulled into the Blackberry Hill Bed and Breakfast, shut off his truck and grabbed the bag beside him on the seat. A few moments later, he was standing in the foyer and handing it to Jenna. "She's not here?"

Jenna shook her head. "She needed to do some

shopping—and she wanted to drive down to the campground to see where she stood. I offered to go along, but she wanted to do it herself."

He got that. The best way to handle lousy news was to face it head-on. Despite her tears last night, she had the strength to do that. "Okay, I'll catch up with her later. I just wanted to drop those off. They're probably the wrong size, but maybe they'll work anyway. The salesclerk said they'd be comfortable." He paused. "Just tell her I—"

A car pulled in outside, and he turned to glance through the screen door. "Never mind," he said, glad to see her red Explorer. "I'll tell her myself."

Blue eyes twinkling, Jenna returned the bag, opened the door and saw him out. "Take your time."

Jake wasn't sure what all that twinkling was about and he didn't ask. He concentrated on Rachel—concentrated on keeping his head straight and their friendship just that. Risking her life to save her wedding portrait from the flames had sent an indelible message. In some ways she would always be David Patterson's wife—and they were ways that counted to a man.

"Hi," she called as she left the car loaded down with packages of her own. It was cool today, but sunlight shot her thick sable shag with highlights. "What brings you to my foster home?"

"Your feet." He was surprised to see her sounding and acting so calm. She looked pretty in the outfit she wore—olive-green cotton slacks and a white sweater with a scooped neckline trimmed in olive-green. He nodded at her new neon-white sneakers as she ascended the steps. "But it looks like you won't need these after all."

With a curious tilt of her head, she accepted the bag he offered. She smiled when she withdrew the shoe box and opened the lid. "Sandals?"

"You can return them if you don't like them or they don't fit. Because I wasn't sure of your size, I sort of—" He positioned his hands this way and that as though he were holding her foot again. "Guessing isn't an exact science."

Her green eyes warmed, and a matching feeling rose in his chest. Then he watched her take a seat on the porch's wicker sofa, ease off her sneakers and short socks and slip on the low-heeled, cushion-soled, strappy leather sandals he'd bought for her. The bandages he'd applied to her left foot last night had been replaced with fresh ones.

"Will they work?" Ridiculous as it seemed, he couldn't recall ever giving a gift that made him feel so... He didn't know what the right word was, but if spending a few bucks made him feel this good, he'd buy footgear for the whole town.

She stood and flashed a foot. "They're great! I love them. I feel like Cinderella."

And he felt like the prince. Although the service revolver on his hip and his tan uniform were a far cry from a plumed hat and a silver sword.

"I have to pay you for them."

"No, you don't. Just consider them a fair trade for six months worth of coffee." He dropped his voice and changed the subject. "How did things go today? Did the fire marshal get in touch with you?"

Sobering, she sat back down and he took a seat beside her. "I haven't heard anything yet. But my insurance company's in the process of putting through the claim."

"That has to be a relief."

"You have no idea," she returned. The light in her eyes dimmed for an instant, then she called up a quick smile. "But I'm good now. I lived through visiting the rubble, so now it's onward and upward."

"You're still planning to open Memorial Day weekend?" He'd walked down to her house today, too, and the smell of charred wood and chemical odors still remained. Yards of yellow police tape couldn't hold back the stench.

"Yes. Thank heaven my guest list and information was in the camp store's computer, too. I was able to phone everyone who'd booked sites and tell them I couldn't guarantee the smoke smell would be gone when they arrived."

Jake smiled inside when she tucked her socks, sneakers and the empty shoe box into the bag, but kept the sandals on her feet.

"Anyway," she continued, "I gave them the option of canceling, but no one wanted to. My business survived. I'm feeling blessed."

"You feel blessed? By God?"

"Well, yes," she said with a grin. "He's the guy in charge of that stuff."

Jake shook his head. "You amaze me."

"Why?"

"Because you're so at peace with everything. So accepting. So positive. It's just hard to understand how you could lose your home and—"

"Watching my home go up in flames was devastating," she assured him. "But there's nothing I can do about it. Would you rather see me crying again?"

"No, but I can't understand why you stopped. You're like my mother. You're devout. You pray, you go to church every Sunday even if you're exhausted. Don't you deserve better than this? Why aren't you mad at God?"

She tilted her head. "Why would I be mad at Him? He saved my life. He woke me up."

"That wasn't God you heard. Your smoke detectors woke you up."

"No, they didn't. I woke up before they went off. But even if I'd had to depend on them, God gave someone the intelligence to invent them, so in the end…"

Jake sighed at her unshakable faith and conceded. She *was* like his mother. Full of forgiveness. "Okay, God woke you up. I got it."

"Good, because it's true."

She got quiet then, and as birds called to each other and the sun slid behind a thick bank of clouds, Jake realized it was time to leave. She had things to do. At the very least, she probably needed some rest.

"You're sure I can't pay you for the sandals?" she asked, rising with him, then joking. "I'll be getting a big insurance check soon, so I can afford it."

"I'm positive." It still astounded him that she could make light of her loss—at least on the surface.

"Then let me thank you another way—for the sandals and for everything you did last night." Her next very familiar words made Jake wonder if he did have his head on straight where she was concerned. "Let me treat you to an early dinner. Nothing fancy. Just chicken at the diner, and maybe ice cream for dessert."

He battled with himself for a few seconds, wondering if saying yes was a good idea. If he started caring too much about someone who was unavailable, he could be running around with a hole in his gut again. He hadn't liked it the first time, and he was pretty sure the second time would be even worse. But…they were friends, and she felt grateful. Nothing more. "Can you wait until I change clothes and check on Maggie?"

"No problem," she said, indicating the outfit she wore. "I have things to do, too. These are Jenna's. I'd like to toss the clothes I bought in the washer before I leave so I can wear my own things tomorrow. I don't want to put her out any more than I have to."

"Okay." But he suspected that Jenna didn't consider herself "put out" at all. "Do you want to meet me at the diner around five?"

"Five's perfect."

"Great. I'll see you then."

He was in his truck and about to pull out of the driveway and onto Main Street Extension when his cell phone pumped out a melody. Pulling it from the case on his belt, he checked the caller's number. And everything inside of him shut down. Drawing a breath, he flipped open the phone and tried to keep his voice polite. Trying was a big fat waste of time.

"Hello, Heather," he said coolly. "What do you want?"

The diner was noisy when they arrived, the chatter of conversation and clank of silverware nearly drowning out the pop music from the seventies. It was Saturday night. The lunch counter was jammed, short tables were pushed together to accommodate parents and kids, and teenagers were packed six in a booth. Three waitresses moved along at a steady clip, trying to keep up. Everyone seemed to be having a good time.

Everyone except Jake, Rachel guessed.

He was trying to hide it, but something had definitely changed since she last saw him. "Where would you like to sit?" she asked. There were a few small tables available in the center of the room, but the booths were all full.

"Anywhere," he said, forcing a friendly grin. "The food will be good no matter where we sit."

But would the conversation be good, too? Especially with the two of them trapped in the middle of madness and mayhem? Rachel's interest sharpened as a couple got up and left a back booth. The table wasn't cleared, but— She turned to Jake and smiled. "Follow me, sir."

Several people offered their sympathies on the fire as they threaded their way back. The women all eyed Jake with subtle interest, which was the nature of things. But their interest wasn't confined to his broad shoulders, jeans and pale blue knit shirt. Rachel knew they wondered if she and Jake were a couple.

By the time they made it to their booth, eighteen-year-old bundle-of-energy Mitzi Abbott had cleared away the glasses and plates. The cute brunette flashed them a smile, spritzed water on the table and whisked a cloth over it.

"Hi, Rachel. Hi, Jake. Do you need menus? Our special's chicken-fried steak with your choice of potato or green beans and either French onion soup or a side salad. Oh, cinnamon applesauce comes with it, too."

"The special sounds good," Jake said, smiling. "I'll have the salad, baked potato and coffee. Rachel?"

"Same here," she said, although she knew it was going to be too much food.

Mitzi was already on the move. "Great," she called. "I'll be right back with your drinks."

Rachel slid into the booth, set her shoulder bag on the seat beside her, then met Jake's eyes across the table. When she didn't say anything for a full moment, he spoke.

"What?"

"Ninety minutes ago you were happy and upbeat. Now you're distracted or disturbed about something."

"It's that obvious?"

"To me it is. Do you want to talk about it? Or should I mind my own business?"

He didn't have time to respond—which might have been a good thing, Rachel decided. A tall, rack-of-bones man with pale blue eyes and rimless eyeglasses left his table and walked on stork legs to their booth. Elmer Fox's red plaid flannel shirt was tucked into navy work pants, and his belt was cinched so tightly that it puckered his waistband. Closely clipped white hair showed under his red-and-black Woolrich cap.

Charity's favorite outspoken octogenarian spoke in a hoarse voice that made people want to clear their throats. "Heard about the fire, Rachel. You doin' all right?"

By now, her responses were all the same. "Yes, I'm doing fine. Thanks for asking."

He folded his long, lanky frame into the booth beside her. "Dang shame. All them firemen working so hard and unable to save your place. I hear you're stayin' at the Blackberry for now."

"Yes. Jenna insisted."

"That's good of her. But you got a campground to run, and it's gonna be hard to do it from town." He paused. "I got a nice room at my place if you want it. It ain't fancy like the Blackberry, but it's clean and it's a dang sight closer to your work."

Rachel's heart nearly melted. What a darling man he was. But there was no way she could accept his offer. Besides, she already had a plan of sorts. She reached over to squeeze his age-spotted hand. "Thank you, but I'm afraid tongues would wag if I moved in with you. I wouldn't want to put you in that position."

For a long moment, Elmer stared at her blankly as if trying to decipher what she meant. Then a light went on in his blue eyes, his jaw dropped and he hooted until he wheezed. "Now wouldn't that be somethin'! Last time folks gossiped about me, Ike was in office."

Laughing along with him, Rachel turned to Jake and made belated introductions. "Jake, do you know Elmer Fox?"

He reached across the table to shake Elmer's hand. "Only by sight and reputation." Which was considerable, Rachel thought. "Nice to meet you, Mr. Fox."

Elmer's expression soured. "You the new game warden?"

"Yep." Technically, he was a W.C.O., but game warden worked.

"You read any of the signs outside my house?"

"Yes, sir, I have. I drive by your place almost daily."

"Then you know I don't like the way you fellas are managing the deer."

Jake seemed to hold back a smile. "I do. Maybe we should talk sometime."

"Maybe we should," he agreed with a grumpy nod. Then he glanced at the table full of teenagers he'd left. Apparently, he'd been holding court. "Well, I gotta get back over there. None of 'em knows a thing about World War II and they got finals coming up."

He shook a finger at Rachel as he started away. "Remember, I got a nice room for you if you want it."

"I'll keep it in mind, Elmer," she called. "Have a nice evening."

Then Mitzi arrived with their drinks and salads, more people stopped by their table to offer their sympathies and talk about the fire and the time for discussing Jake's problem passed.

He surprised her by following her back to the Blackberry after they'd said goodbye at the diner—then thoroughly stunned her with an invitation.

"Feel like taking a drive?" he said when he'd parked and exited his vehicle.

A drive? Now? It would be dark in two hours. "Sure," she said after a moment. "Is there something you want to talk about?"

He nodded. "Yeah. Heather called."

SIX

Payton's Rocks was the highest point in the area, filled with a craggy kind of beauty, its gigantic rock formations nearly scraping the sky. Jake's tires crunched over dirt and gravel as they came to a stop and he shut off the motor.

"I stumbled onto this place shortly after I transferred," he said as they exited the vehicle. "I'm always surprised that there aren't more people using the resources up here."

"I'm not," Rachel returned as they walked, single file, over the narrow path to the rocks. She didn't mind their small talk. When he was ready to discuss that phone call, he would. "I think it's fairly common for people to miss the beauty in their own backyards. My dad calls it 'the grass is greener syndrome.'"

He spoke from behind her. "How's your dad doing?"

"Getting stronger every day, and I'm so thankful."

"Did you tell your mom and dad about the fire?"

"No, and I hope no one else does, either, until I have something positive to add."

"Rebuilding is positive."

"I know, but that won't happen for a while." Contractors would have their work lined up by now, probably into the fall.

The path opened wide enough for them to walk side-by-side, then wider still until they were finally staring at centuries-old rock behemoths. They strolled among the giants for a while, marveling at the size and mass of the rocks, then finally settled on a low, sun-warmed boulder surrounded by blue sky. Far below, cutting through the heavily forested hillside, the state route they'd traveled was a winding gray ribbon.

"About Heather..." he said when he'd been silent for a while. "I still can't believe she called. After the way we left it, I didn't think I'd ever hear from her again."

"Your parting wasn't friendly."

He blew out a short laugh. "Not even a little bit. I probably should have changed my cell phone number."

"What did she want?" It was hardly her place to ask, but that question had been burning in her mind since he'd uttered Heather's name twenty minutes ago.

"She says she wants to visit."

Rachel's pulse stepped up its pace, and glancing down, she zipped Jenna's blue fleece jacket, suddenly needing to do something with her hands. "How do you feel about that?"

"Not great." He scooped up a few pebbles, then stood and arced one after another over the precipice to the forest below. "Did I tell you she worked for a travel agency?"

"No," she replied quietly. "You never even mentioned her name until a few minutes ago."

"Well, that's how we met. My parents were taking another cruise, and my dad asked me to pick up the tickets. He'd booked with Heather several times and really liked her. Somewhere along the line, I guess he decided that if we met..."

He didn't finish, so she finished for him. "The two of you would click?"

"Something like that." He scooped up a few more pebbles, then sent them flying, as well. "Long story short, it worked for a while. Then her boss divorced his wife, and Heather decided Mark was more exciting than a guy who wanted to live and work in the woods. According to her, a guy who had no desire to live up to his potential."

Stunned that any woman would leave Jake for any reason—particularly when she knew who and what he was when they met—Rachel took a moment to reply. "I'm not sure I understand," she said.

"My family's half owner of Prestige Communications. You've probably heard of it."

Who hadn't? Rachel thought, startled. Prestige wasn't as big as AT&T or Comcast, but it was sizable.

"Prestige supplies broadband service to several hundred thousand customers. Maybe more now. I don't ask. Anyway...Heather wanted me to take a position in the company—which would have made my dad ecstatic, too. But that's not who I am, or who I ever wanted to be. She didn't get it."

"Did your dad 'get it'?"

"If you mean, was he upset when I didn't come aboard after college, no." Jake tossed the last pebble, then dusted his hands and turned back to her. "He understood that I needed to do what made me happy—although that's probably because he does have a son at the business. My brother, Greg, and his wife both work at Prestige."

Rachel remained silent, still trying to wrap her mind around Jake's life. They'd known each other for six months and he'd never mentioned that his family was wealthy—and by extension, that he was, too. She wouldn't have guessed that from the simple way he lived.

"When Heather finally realized where we'd be living, who our friends would be and, more importantly, that we wouldn't be jetting off to Europe or the Bahamas a dozen times a year, her interest shifted. Mark—her boss—had always had a thing for her. But I trusted her, and he was married." He shrugged. "I guess she got tired of living vicariously through her clients. She slept with Mark, he bought her a black Corvette and I said adios."

Rachel spoke softly. "Oh, Jake, I'm sorry."

He looked at her, his gaze grim. "Yeah. For a while, I was one flat tire and an old dog shy of a country song. Now she wants to visit me."

"Does she…?" Rachel drew a breath, startled by the sudden racing of her heart. "Does she want you back?"

"I don't know."

"Do you want her back?"

He couldn't have sounded more certain. "Absolutely not."

Still…he'd been thrown by that phone call, and when she'd asked how he felt about Heather visiting, he'd been vague.

Late that night, once again unable to sleep, Rachel stared at the ceiling from her bed at the Blackberry. And she and her fluttering stomach wondered if there was still unfinished business between Jake and the woman who'd betrayed him.

Her stomach didn't feel much better after the fire marshal visited her the next day. He stayed only long enough to deliver disturbing news that no one should hear on a sunny Sunday morning. Then he left her in Chief Lon Perris's hands.

Rachel sank to the sofa on Jenna's porch, her knees suddenly weak. Behind her, Jenna squeezed Rachel's shoulder.

"Arson?" Rachel said in a barely audible voice. She met Chief Perris's steely gaze. "You're absolutely certain?"

Perris glanced beyond the Blackberry's porch to the parking area where a state police cruiser was just pulling out. In Pennsylvania, the fire marshal was a state police officer. "It's not my job or expertise to be certain." He nodded at the car. "But it is his, and he says it was an accelerant fire. We need to talk about that because it's obvious from the circumstances that someone wants you dead."

Chills drizzled through her. "Who?"

"That's what we have to figure out. Do you know of anyone who might want to do you harm? Enemies—past or present—who have a problem with you?"

"No," she said numbly. "I—I don't have enemies."

Perris pressed on. "A disgruntled campground guest? A vendor? Someone you turned away because of prior bad behavior?"

Rachel shook her head. She got along with everyone,

and she'd never had occasion to ask any of her campers to leave. "No. No, there's no one."

"There has to be. Think. Even the most innocent remark or trivial occurrence could set off the wrong person."

Rachel released a shaky sigh. "Look, would you like me to make up something? Because that's the only way you're going to get a name from me."

Jenna moved around the sofa to face Perris, her brow lining. "You need to know something about Rachel. She's the closest thing we have in Charity to a saint."

"Jen, please."

"Hush. It's the truth." She spoke to the chief again. "She goes to church, she helps out at the nursing home—despite the fact that she has more than enough work of her own to do—and she's the first in line to volunteer when a friend or neighbor needs a hand. If someone wants to hurt her—"

"There is no *if*," Perris said. "It's a sure thing."

"Then it's someone neither of us knows," Jenna stated emphatically. "Maybe the fire was random. Maybe—"

"That's highly unlikely, but I'm not ruling anything out." He directed his remarks to Rachel again. "In the meantime, it would be best if you kept your stay here a secret."

She would have laughed if the situation hadn't been so grave. "A secret in Charity? There *are* no secrets in Charity. I suspect Hector at the post office has already filled out a change of address card for me to sign."

"Then I suggest that you limit your wanderings and keep thinking about people you might have offended, because there is someone out there."

Rachel got to her feet. "I can't stay here forever. My campground will be opening soon, and there's still work to be done."

Perris responded sharply. "Then you'd better hire some security because we don't know who this monkey is or what motivates him. If the person who torched your house is the same man you saw last Sunday night, he's got an agenda and he's dedicated. Do you know what I mean by *dedicated?*"

She nodded. "He won't stop."

"That's right."

Jenna touched her arm. "I think hiring a couple of men to keep an eye on the campground is a very good idea. In fact, Joe Reston came by yesterday to see if I needed help. He and a few others were laid off at the lumber mill Friday, and he's looking for work until things pick up." She paused to make a point. "He's big and he's intimidating."

True, Rachel thought. He was also the first man she'd considered while trying to put a face on her intruder.

A dark blue Ram truck sped up the drive and parked next to Perris's prowl car. Seconds later, Jake got out and walked toward the porch. Rachel's thankful heart leaped. The cavalry had arrived. Not a whole troop. Just one man in jeans, boots and a chambray shirt with the sleeves rolled back over his muscular forearms. A man who made her feel safe just by being here.

Jenna spoke quietly. "He asked me to call him as soon as you heard the fire marshal's findings. I didn't think you'd mind."

Rachel nodded. She didn't mind at all.

Jake took the steps to the wide wraparound porch, his expression lined. After nodding to Perris, he thanked

Jenna for calling and met Rachel's eyes. "Are you okay?"

"As okay as anyone would be after making a fire-bug's hit list."

Mouth thinning, Perris turned to Jake. "Convince her to lay low for a while. I can have an officer drive by here more often, but the department's too small for much more than that." He cut a look at Rachel. "Call the station if anything unusual happens or if you come up with a name for me. I'll contact you when I have something to report."

Rachel nodded and expressed her thanks, glad to be on friendlier terms with the man. Well…if not friendlier, at least tolerable terms.

When the chief had gone and Jenna had stepped inside to dress for church, Jake spoke somberly. "I hope you're not taking this as lightly as it sounded—or as lightly as Perris thinks you are."

"I'm not. I'm scared. I just don't see much value in running around, wringing my hands."

"Good. Then you *will* sit tight?"

Rachel hesitated. She'd been turning things around in her mind ever since the fire marshal had given her the verdict, and she'd come up with several undeniable facts. None of which allowed her to "sit tight," no matter how frightened she was. She indicated the sweat pants and T-shirt she wore, clothes she'd pulled from her dryer the night of the fire. "Can we talk about this later? I need to get dressed for church."

His jaw dropped. "You're going to church?"

"It's Sunday. I go to church on Sundays."

"This isn't about your faith, Rachel," he said, his frustration evident. "It's about your safety."

She swallowed, believing the words she was about to say, though she wasn't crazy about the prospect. "None of us leaves this world until God says it's time to go. If He decides it's my time, locking doors and hiding here at Jenna's won't do me any good."

Jake's mood didn't improve with her rationale. "That doesn't mean you have to deliberately put yourself in harm's way. I thought the Lord helped those who help themselves. Or don't you agree?"

"I do, but I need to be in church today, Jake. I need to. No one's going to hurt me there."

He seemed to consider that for a long moment, then nodded. But his stoic look and the gravity in his eyes told her he didn't like her decision. "What time's the service?"

"Eleven o'clock."

"Then you'd better get moving," he said, glancing at his wristwatch. "It's already ten-twenty-five."

An hour and a half later, Rachel shook hands with Reverend Landers and followed Jenna and a friend of hers out of St. John's Church. Dressed in his collar and Sunday blacks, Landers was a warm, elderly man with white hair, a bit of a potbelly and kind blue eyes behind rimless bifocals. Inside, Emma Lucille Bridger was still pounding on the organ, the last swelling strains of "Amazing Grace" rolling into the street.

"The service was lovely," Rachel said, smiling. "It was exactly what I needed today."

He took her hand in both of his. "I'm glad. I wasn't sure we'd see you this morning. How are you holding up? Is there anything more we can do for you—other than prayer?"

"Probably not," she replied, wondering if she should mention the fire marshal's findings before it became common knowledge. "Just keep the prayers coming and I'll be fine."

The tall man behind her begged to differ. "She'd be a lot finer if she took the advice the police gave her."

Landers's curious glance slid between them, and Rachel shot Jake a look. The "wondering" was over. She didn't want to talk about the fire. Not after the music, the lesson and the hymns had managed to dull her fears a little. "Reverend Landers," she said, "I'd like you to meet my friend and neighbor Jake Campbell. Jake's a wildlife conservation officer."

Jake gripped the hand Landers extended. "Nice to meet you, Reverend."

"Likewise. Actually, I believe I saw you talking with Rachel the night of the fire. I hope you enjoyed the service today, Mr. Campbell."

"I did. And it's Jake."

"Good. Then maybe we'll see you again, Jake?"

He hesitated. "Maybe." He glanced at Rachel's dress, then took in the attire of a few of the congregation who were talking a short distance away. "I hope you'll forgive the way I'm dressed, Reverend. Attending was a last-minute decision."

"The Lord doesn't care how you're dressed, son," Landers replied, chuckling. "He just wants you to show up. Right, Rachel?"

She smiled. "Right." Low voices behind her alerted her that a few stragglers were on their way out of the church, and she nodded toward the parking lot. "Thanks again for the prayers, Reverend. See you next Sunday."

"Enjoy the day, you two," he said. "The Lord's given us a good one."

"That's a matter of opinion," Jake said as they walked across the grass to the parking lot. He kept his attention moving, scanning, presumably watching for firebugs. "How good can a day be when it starts out with a word like arson?"

Rachel didn't comment. She didn't want to get into it right now. Incredible as it seemed, she was hungry, and if she started focusing on what could happen to her, she'd never be able to eat a thing. Head-hiding ostriches had the right idea. "Do you want to join Jenna at the diner for the Sunday brunch? My treat. Or would you rather just drop me off at the Blackberry?"

"I'd *rather* take you home and handcuff you to a chair until Perris and the staties figure out who torched your house. But I'll settle for driving you to my place until Jenna comes back."

"I'm hungry, Jake. I nee—"

"Then you're in luck. I have food."

"Okay," he said, when Maggie was chewing steak bones in the weeds and quack grass he called a yard. They carried their iced teas to the front porch's wooden swing and took a seat. "Let's talk about your business." She'd grown quiet after they'd eaten, and he suspected the reality of what she was up against had finally hit her. She could talk all day about having no choice in God's decisions, but beneath her rationalizations she was afraid it might just *be* her time.

She studied her iced tea. "Okay, what about my business?"

Jake felt his sympathies multiply. Where she'd

seemed strong in her sweats and T-shirt, her new gauzy, pale green dress printed with tiny pink flowers made her look soft and vulnerable. It was belted, and above her round neckline, he could see her pulse beating. Her throat was bare, without the gold cross she usually wore. Then he realized it had probably been lost in the fire.

"Jenna said Perris suggested that you hire a few security guys to walk the property."

She nodded. "Yes, and it was a good suggestion. I can't afford any more vandalism with my guests and summer help coming in soon. I don't want anyone hurt because I didn't take precautions."

"I agree." The swing's chains creaked a little as he touched his boot to the floor and set the swing in lazy motion.

"I think I can get away with hiring only three men, one per eight-hour shift. Maybe one more to fill in so the original three can have a day off. Hopefully, with my summer help, that will be enough of a presence to discourage anyone from doing something stupid."

He'd placed a parson's stool in front of them, and he swallowed tea before setting his glass down on it. "If you're worried that that could happen, maybe you should close the campground until this is over."

"I can't. Despite the situation, my guests want to come. I did call my competitors and asked if they could squeeze a few of them in if that wasn't the case. But it's the first camping weekend of the summer, and everyone's full." She paused "You know, I've been thinking. The intruder didn't threaten me personally. He went after Tim's equipment. So if the two events are connected, maybe the fire isn't about settling a grudge or someone hating me. Maybe it's about something else."

He'd considered that, too, mostly because he couldn't imagine anyone even disliking her. "It might be. But burning down your house in the middle of the night's pretty extreme if the man just wants to ruin you financially."

"I know. And I can't think of anyone who'd want to do that. As I said, the other campgrounds are full, too. The elk herd and local attractions draw people here. There's plenty of business for everyone."

A gray SUV appeared at the top of his driveway, then rolled down to the house and parked behind Jake's truck. Barking, Maggie jumped up from the lawn and stood at rigid attention when Ben Caruthers got out. She kept it up until Jake ordered her to stay.

"Afternoon, Rachel," Ben called. "Hi, Jake."

They both called back greetings as Ben crossed the yard. Maggie beat him to the porch, then sat sentinel between Jake and Rachel, nearly tipping over their drinks on the parson's table. A low growl rumbled in her throat.

"Enough, Maggie," Jake ordered. "Lie down."

"Pretty dog," Ben said, climbing the steps, then leaning against the post. The balding hardware store owner was dressed in navy slacks and a crisp, blue plaid cotton shirt—a far cry from the smoke-smudged bunker pants and suspenders he'd worn the other night. "I had a setter a few years back, too," he continued. "She was a good girl, but a little too high-strung for me."

"Yeah, that's the story on them," Jake returned. "Especially the pups and young ones. Maggie's usually pretty mellow, but then, she's nearly five." He motioned to one of the two Adirondack chairs he intended to refinish. “Have a seat. Can I get you something to drink? Rachel made iced tea.”

“No, thanks, I just wanted to see how she was getting along.” His round face lined compassionately as he shifted his gaze to Rachel. “I stopped by the Blackberry to see you, but Jenna said you’d gone with Jake after church. So…here I am. Anything I can do to make this easier on you? Other than offer you a discount on whatever you need from my store when you decide to rebuild?”

She smiled. “Thanks. That’s nice. As for anything beyond a discount… I wish you could do something, but no. Unless you want to join my security team.”

He glanced between Jake and Rachel. “Security team?”

“Yes. I’m concerned that there could be more trouble, so I’m hiring a few men to watch over my campground until I move back. Maybe longer.”

Jake felt himself still inside. Something in her voice hinted that she wouldn’t be living in town for long. “What do you mean ‘until you move back’?”

She turned to him. “I can’t stay with Jenna forever, taking up space that she could rent to someone. And I can’t supervise my business through a telescope. I need to be down here.”

Ben’s high forehead lined, and he crossed the porch to the seat Jake had offered. “All things considered, is that wise? After the fire marshal’s findings, I’d hoped you’d shut your campground down for a while. I don’t want to alarm you any further, but going back there before the police have someone in custody could be very risky.”

“I realize that,” she returned. “But I can’t close when

so many people are looking forward to their trips—some of whom have arranged to be off work or school. It's almost too late for them to change their plans." She drew a squiggle in the condensation on her glass. "All I know for sure is, I need to get what's left of my house cleared away as soon as possible. I'm hoping Tim can handle that, too."

Jake leaned forward on the swing to face her. "Too? Then you're going ahead with the golf course? With everything else you have on your plate?"

"There's no reason not to. Most of it's already paid for, and Tim's set aside time for the job. He called before the fire marshal showed up this morning."

"Oh?"

She nodded. "He said I could bail out if I wanted to—that he might be able to pick up another job. But what if he couldn't? I'd be costing him work. I told him I wanted to go ahead as planned." She smiled a little. "As of Tuesday, his other dozer will be available. He should be able to start again soon."

Ben spoke. "Don't you have to clear that with the police first?"

"I don't think so, but I'll look into it. The site's well beyond the area the police taped off."

"Then I guess that's good news." He checked his watch, then planted his hands on the chair's arms and levered himself up. "Where will you stay when you move back?" he asked, moving toward the steps.

"Good question. With all of my cabins reserved, I'll probably have to buy or rent a travel trailer. There's no point moving into one of the A-frames when I'll just have to move again in two weeks." She smiled tightly. "I guess I'm still figuring that out." Rising, she walked him to his vehicle, Jake and Maggie joining them belatedly.

"Well," Ben said, giving Rachel a long, hard hug. "If you think of anything I can do to help, I'm your guy." Climbing inside, he continued to speak through his open window. "That is, anything other than joining your security team. I still have a hardware store to run."

"Not for long, though, right?" Rachel replied. "A little bird told me you might be moving to Phoenix to be closer to your son."

"Not anymore," he returned, his smile growing. "Randy's coming back home. The office rat race finally got to him. I'll be adding 'and Son' to the sign outside my shop."

"Ben, that's great."

"I think so, too. I wouldn't have been good in that heat. And I would have missed the change of seasons." He turned the key, then frowned as if something had suddenly occurred to him. "You know, if you're ready to go back to town, I can drop you off at the Blackberry and save Jake a trip. I have to pass it on my way home anyway."

Jake spoke before she could accept. "Thanks, but I'll take her back in a little while."

"Yes, thank you," Rachel repeated, sending Jake a curious look. "And thanks for the visit."

"Anytime. See you again soon."

When the SUV had turned onto the rural route and they were returning to the porch, Rachel glanced up at him. "I understand your need to be…vigilant…but I could've gone with him. He's safe. I'm sure you have other things you could be doing besides running a taxi service."

Jake kept his gaze straight ahead. "At the moment, I don't," he said, his mind's eye still seeing Ben's arms around Rachel. "Besides, I thought you wanted to check on your store and outbuildings again before you went back to town." That had been the first order of business when they'd gotten here. "Or have you changed your mind?"

"No, but Ben wouldn't have had a problem stopping there for a few minutes. He's a good guy. It was nice of him to offer to save you a trip."

"Yeah, well, he's too old for you." The second the words were out, Jake wanted to snatch them back and stuff them down a mine shaft. What was going on with him? This was the second time in a week that he'd said something that was totally at odds with who he was.

She shot him a startled look. "What?"

"Nothing," he said, irritated with himself. "Let's finish our iced tea and take that walk."

They didn't leave right away. She'd insisted on helping him stain his chairs to thank him for lunch, so it was nearly dusk and a light breeze had picked up when they finally drove down to the store.

Despite his protests, he couldn't keep her away from her burned-out home. Like that proverbial moth to a flame, she needed to see again for herself what was left. Overnight, even that partial stone chimney had toppled, and when she saw it, tears filled her eyes.

Jake could only imagine what was going through her mind. The home she'd shared with her late-husband was gone, just as he was. Now she really was on her own. Her tears began to roll.

"Don't cry," he said softly.

Her voice was barely audible. "I'm not."

"Yes, I can see that," he said, slipping his arms around her. She felt small. Small and sad and beautiful and lost, and suddenly he just couldn't handle her unhappiness. He tipped her face up to his. "It's going to be okay," he murmured over her sobs. "You'll get through this. You're strong."

"What if I'm not strong enough?"

"I'll help you. You know that." Then he couldn't concentrate on anything but her wide green eyes and the soft lips that were so close to his. With a breathy sigh, he covered them with his own. He kept the kiss gentle... tasted her softness and her tears, felt himself melt into her when she kissed him back. Then he slowly eased away and she opened her eyes. They still shone with tears, but the sadness, the bleak look he'd seen in them moments ago seemed to have ebbed a little.

"I should get back," she murmured after a moment. "I don't want Jenna to worry."

Jake nodded. "Is there anything you want from your store before we go?" It was a stupid thing to say, but he needed to say something. Because even though he hadn't planned for the kiss to happen, he'd taken advantage of her vulnerability and he didn't know how she felt about that. "A pair of flip-flops? Antiseptic spray? More bandages?"

She smiled. "No, I have a great pair of sandals, and there's enough gauze and antiseptic spray at Jenna's to stock a small pharmacy."

"Well, then," he said, wiping a tear from her cheek. "Let's get you back to the Blackberry."

They were nearly there when a familiar black Corvette sped past them in the opposite lane and pulled into the motor lodge a half mile from the bed and breakfast. Jake's mind played back the blurry image of long blond hair and gold hoop earrings...and tightening his grip on the steering wheel, he continued toward the Blackberry and waited for his cell phone to ring.

SEVEN

Jake said good-night to Rachel without apologizing for the kiss. He wasn't sorry and he knew she'd see that in his eyes. Then he put the pedal to the metal and headed for the Tall Spruce Travel Lodge to confront the past that was intruding on his present. It didn't take him long to get there.

The building was a berry-and-tan two-story affair with room entrances off a long upstairs walkway, and a courtyard on the ground floor. Landscape lighting lit the freshly applied red mulch and bushy perennials surrounding the towering blue spruce out front, but the flower beds were still empty. The neon sign above the downstairs office said they had a vacancy.

Swinging out of the truck, Jake made an attempt to bank his agitation and crossed the asphalt to the office. A short, thin kid with a diamond stud earring and a blond faux-hawk smiled from behind the reservations counter. His name tag read Aaron Bridger, and the diamond stud in his ear was just as faux as his long, updated hairstyle.

"Good evening, sir. How can I help?"

"Good evening. I'd like the room number of the young woman who just checked in. Heather Quinn."

The kid gave the expected reply. "I'm sorry, sir. I can't give out that information. Privacy laws prevent—"

"Okay," Jake returned casually, refusing to be turned away. "I'll just knock on a few doors until I find her." When the kid blanched, he went on. "Or you could buzz her room and tell her that Jake Campbell is in the lobby and would like to talk to her. If she says no and makes a fuss, you can call the police. But she's in town to see me."

His proposition appeared to make sense to the kid.

A minute later, Jake climbed the concrete steps to the second floor and took the walkway to room 214. She was waiting for him with the door partially open. She looked beautiful—but then, she always did—in a silky peach-colored tracksuit, with her wavy, thick ash-blond hair tousled and falling over her shoulders.

"Hi," she said with a quiet smile. Opening the door wider, she stepped back to allow him access. "Please come in."

"No, thanks," he said coldly. "This won't take long. I only have one thing to say." He didn't wait for her to ask what it was. "Go home."

Then he turned and left. He was down the stairs and walking back to his vehicle when she called to him from the railing upstairs. "It didn't take you long to move on, did it? Who was the girl in your truck, Jake?"

He didn't slow his stride and he didn't turn around. So she'd seen Rachel. Good. As for it not taking him long to move on… She'd moved on a lot faster than he did. She was still wearing his ring when she accepted the keys to that black Corvette.

Pulling out of the lot, he clicked on his high beams

and headed for home. He was slowly gaining respect for all those tired old adages. What was good for the goose really was good for the gander. And vice versa.

Rachel drew a stabilizing breath, aware that her blood was racing. She watched Jenna fill a copper teakettle from the spigot, then put it on the back burner and adjust the flame beneath it. Several feet away, the table in the kitchen's little breakfast nook was set for the morning's meal. "She said her name was Heather?"

"Yes. Heather Quinn," she replied, facing Rachel again. "She said she was in town to see Jake, and she wanted a room."

"What did you tell her?"

"I said I couldn't accommodate her because I was closed until tomorrow, and as of tomorrow, I was full for several days. Then she asked if there were other B & Bs nearby. That's when I suggested the Tall Spruce. It wasn't her cup of tea, but she asked me to phone the lodge to see if they had a vacancy. They did, so I asked the night clerk to hold it for her. She left in a shiny black Corvette."

Rachel went stone-still. She'd seen that car less than fifteen minutes ago. The headlights had nearly blinded her as it raced up the hill toward the travel lodge. She'd also caught a glimpse of the driver's long blond hair. Slowly, she walked to Jenna, stopping at the butcher block island in the middle of the kitchen. It was a quiet night, and music from the Party Place—the local teens' favorite haunt in the woods up the road—floated through the window screen and the recently added wide, exterior mesh.

"Let me guess. She's beautiful and she's blonde."

Jenna sent her a knowing look. "She's Jake's ex, isn't she?"

Rachel nodded.

"That's what I thought. She seemed too eager to get in touch with him. And to answer your question, she's average-looking." She drew an apologetic breath and went on. "Rachel, she looked at a phone book while she was here. Jake's number wasn't listed because he's so new to the area, so she asked if I knew where he lived."

A tiny ball of apprehension formed in Rachel's stomach, but she nodded her understanding. "It's okay. I wouldn't have expected you to lie." And there was no reason for Jenna *to* lie. She and Jake weren't a couple.

So why did it feel like they were?

Jenna smoothed a lock of blond hair behind her ear. "I didn't lie. But I wasn't sure Jake would want her to know where he lived, so I said I couldn't help her. I think she assumed I didn't know his address, and I didn't correct the assumption." She hesitated. "How do you feel about her being here?"

Rachel glanced away. She had no idea how she felt about it, but her heart was pounding, so she decided she must have some opinion. Especially because her lips still tingled when she remembered his mouth on hers, and she felt a glow recalling the comforting strength of his arms. "I think you were wise not to give out personal information."

"That's not what I asked."

"I know," she murmured. She fished two orange spice tea bags from a canister while Jenna pulled cups and saucers from a white oak cabinet. "You won't believe this, but today of all days, he finally opened up about their breakup." She unwrapped the tea bags, then tucked them into the cups. "Without going into a lot of detail, she slept with someone while they were engaged. Based on that, I don't like her being here, and I don't like her personally. But she is here, and I suspect that Jake has already gone to see her."

Jenna took a bone china sugar bowl from the sideboard and set it beside their cups. "Why do you think that?"

"Because we passed her on the way here, and if I noticed a black Corvette with a lot of long blond hair flying out the open window, so did he."

Jenna's expression softened. "Are you going to talk to him about it?"

"Not unless he brings it up."

"But?"

"But he's been hurt enough. He doesn't need a second helping."

Jenna turned off the teakettle before it could whistle, then poured boiling water over their tea bags. She met Rachel's eyes. "He's not the only one who's been hurt, so be careful. You've handled some serious losses with more courage and acceptance than I ever could have. I don't want to see you take on any more."

Shrugging, Rachel mustered a smile. "I'll be okay." She had to be. She didn't have any choice.

She awoke Monday morning like a whirlwind on steroids, eager to arrange the security at the campground and prepare for her opening. Last night as she lay in bed paging through the Bible from the nightstand in her room, she'd felt the emotional ball in her stomach ease with every joyful passage she read in the psalms. And

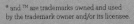

The Reader Service—Here's How It Works:

Accepting your 2 free books and 2 free gifts (gifts valued at approximately $10.00) places you under no obligation to buy anything. You may keep the bo and gifts and return the shipping statement marked "cancel." If you do not cancel, about a month later we will send you 4 additional books and bill you $4.49 each for the regular-print edition or $4.99 each for the larger-print edition in the U.S. or $4.99 each for the regular-print edition or $5.49 each for larger-print edition in Canada. That is a savings of at least 22% off the cover price. It's quite a bargain! Shipping and handling is just 50¢ per book in the and 75¢ per book in Canada.* You may cancel at any time, but if you choose to continue, every month we'll send you 4 more books, which you may eit purchase at the discount price or return to us and cancel your subscription.

*Terms and prices subject to change without notice. Prices do not include applicable taxes. Sales tax applicable in N.Y. Canadian residents will be char applicable taxes. Offer not valid in Quebec. All orders subject to credit approval. Credit or debit balances in a customer's account(s) may be offset by other outstanding balance owed by or to the customer. Please allow 4 to 6 weeks for delivery. Offer available while quantities last.

If offer card is missing write to: The Reader Service, P.O. Box 1867, Buffalo, NY 14240-1867 or visit www.ReaderService.com

NO POSTAGE
NECESSARY
IF MAILED
IN THE
UNITED STATES

BUSINESS REPLY MAIL
FIRST-CLASS MAIL PERMIT NO. 717 BUFFALO, NY
POSTAGE WILL BE PAID BY ADDRESSEE

THE READER SERVICE
PO BOX 1867
BUFFALO NY 14240-9952

she'd prayed hard that God would give her the strength and peace to put her life in His hands. She prayed for contentment and an accepting soul. She knew that could only happen if she gave everything that hurt or angered or frightened her to God. Today, she was making some headway.

By nine-thirty, she'd spoken to Joe Reston, who'd accepted the job, and given her the names of two men who'd also be happy for any work she could send their way. That's what she told Jake when he phoned minutes afterward.

"Where are you interviewing them? At the Blackberry?"

"No, at my store."

"Rachel—"

"It's okay," she assured him, part of her happy to hear the concern in his voice, part of her slightly bothered to have her independence stifled. "I won't be alone. I'm meeting the guys there at eleven, and the Pepsi distributor's sending someone to fill the pop machines around noon."

He mumbled something she couldn't make out, then spoke again. "I'm in the field now, but I should be finished around four. Will you be at the store?"

"Yes," she replied with a patient smile. "So will Joe Reston. He'll start at three."

"And between noon and three?"

She sighed. "Between noon and three, God will watch out for me. Now I really have to go, Jake. I have a lot to do."

When she left the B & B at ten to drive to her camp store, she felt like things were falling into place. Tim Decker would start clearing the land tomorrow morning,

Jake seemed just as caring as he'd been last night despite Heather's arrival and she'd made a sensible decision about her living arrangements. She was vacuuming the indoor-outdoor carpeting in the store's game room at eleven o'clock when Joe and the Atkins brothers, Roy and Wes, came inside. The Atkinses were average-size men in jeans, boots and T-shirts, and both of them sported short dark hair and trimmed beards. Lady Killer Joe was another story. His hair was a rust-red mullet, and his tight white muscle shirt showed his thick neck, broad chest and bulging biceps to advantage. *Her* advantage. Few intruders would consider mixing it up with a man who stood six-feet-four in his boots, even if he did wear a gold necklace and too much cologne.

It took less than ten minutes to orient them. The only thing they were expected to do was patrol the loops using the golf cart from the utility shed, and make sure all was well. For now, they'd use the number three cabin as their base of operations. Joe would begin at three. Other than that, the men could schedule their shifts. With Tim Decker coming back tomorrow—and leaving his equipment—she didn't want a repeat of last week's vandalism.

As for Joe… Deep down, Rachel still worried a little that hiring him was like asking the fox to guard the henhouse. But she needed to secure the campground, he was available and Jake doubted that Joe was her prowler.

When she'd handed Joe the cabin key, and the guys had agreed that what she'd pay them was fair, she smiled and shook their hands. "Now," she said, "if you don't have to run off right away, I could really use your help moving a few things around in my game room."

* * *

Grim faced, Jake glanced around and shook his head. The pool table and Space Trek arcade game had been moved aside to accommodate some sort of bed. Nothing had changed at the opposite side of the room where the TV was ringed by chairs and a small sofa. An Xbox and selection of video games, books, board games and activities for younger campers filled the bookshelf beside the folded card table.

He looked her squarely in the eyes. She was completely out of her mind. "This is your plan?"

She lifted her chin defensively. "Yes, and I can see by the look on your face that you don't think it's a very good one."

"Rachel, you can't live here."

"I can, and I will until I make other arrangements. I'd rather not buy a travel trailer right now with the insurance claim pending."

"But you won't have any privacy, there's no bathroom to speak of—"

"I have a restroom," she said, crisply gesturing to it as she strode back into the store and galley area. "This is a solid structure. I have a roof over my head, a door I can shut, and I'm usually here until closing at ten o'clock anyway."

She moved behind the lunch counter and grabbed a dish cloth to wipe the already-clean blue Formica countertop. Jake decided she did it to put space between them. He lowered himself to one of the blue vinyl stools across from her.

"There's no room in there."

"I don't need a lot of space."

"But you do need *some*." He understood that she

wanted a place of her own. And now that she'd hired men to patrol the campground, she wouldn't be alone. But it felt like she was moving into a cardboard box and still needed a pair of mismatched shoes and a heavy muffler for the coming winter. "What are you going to do for a shower?"

"I have two bathhouses. One for men, one for women, and there's plenty of hot water. I can take soap, shampoo and anything else I'll need right off my shelves." She stopped wiping, did a little turnaround to show off her new jeans and Patterson's Campground T-shirt, then went back to work. "That includes my wardrobe."

He shook his head. "You're not thinking this through. Where will you put your clothes? Where will you go when you need some time out from your guests and the pressure of running the campground? I wasn't here last summer, but I assume your summer help worked in the store a few hours a day to give you a break. Or are you telling me you never went to your house to kick back and relax for a few minutes?"

When her backbone slumped and her defensiveness ebbed, he felt lousy, but she needed to be realistic.

"I'm not saying that at all," she replied, her voice still strong. "I'm just telling you that I have a plan I can work with for a few days or weeks, and I'd appreciate it if you'd stop poking holes in it. It's tough enough to stay positive with my home in ashes and a target on my back."

"Rachel, I didn't mean to do that, and I know how difficult—" He blew out a breath and stopped. No, he didn't know how difficult it was because no one had threatened his life and his home was still in one piece.

"Okay. I'm sorry. What do you need to make this work?"

"A bed. I need a decent inflatable mattress, a pillow and a sleeping bag—or even better, a roll-away cot that I can store during the day and use at night. I stock air mattresses for the pool, but I need something that will hold up."

"Okay. When do you want to shop?"

"Ten minutes ago."

Jake got up from the stool, walked around the counter and took the dishcloth from her hand—tossed it in the sink behind her. Even though she was in knots today, she looked pretty with her hair fringing her high cheekbones and dark-lashed green eyes. "Come on," he said. "Let's lock up and go shopping."

The sprawling department store in the mall fifteen miles from Charity was open 24-7, and teeming with customers at five-thirty. They didn't sell roll-away cots, but they did have a nice assortment of sleeping bags and thick air mattresses. Rachel found a queen-sized mattress that appealed to her, along with a mattress pad, sheets, a sleeping bag and a pillow. As long as she was shopping, she added a selection of fresh produce and a few health-and-beauty items to her cart. Jake followed her around with an anvil on his chest. She was having fun choosing the necessities she'd need—almost as if she were preparing for a camping trip, not a new lifestyle she'd been thrust into. But he didn't like it. He didn't like it at all.

Rachel hesitated as she approached the women's clothing department. "Do you mind if I grab a few more things? I won't be long."

"No problem," he said. "Take your time. If it's all right with you, afterward I have a quick stop to make. Do you like Mexican food?"

An hour later at the camp store, they filled up on fajitas and honey-dipped sopapillas, then Jake helped her put her new "bedroom" together. Images floated through his mind as he inflated her air mattress, and every one of them gave him a bad feeling. He pictured her having microwave popcorn for breakfast—saw her with a flashlight in her hand trying to read at night. And he imagined her picking up her inflatable bed and jamming it into a corner when she woke up before she could open for her guests. His total dislike of the situation made it impossible to keep his mouth shut.

"You should stay at Jenna's until you absolutely have to be here," he said as they walked to the door and he prepared to follow her back to Charity. "You're not going to be comfortable. You need to reconsider."

"Jacob," she said evenly, "let's not do this again."

Jacob? "What am I doing?"

"You know what you're doing. I'm a big girl. I'll be thirty-three in a few days, and I survived on my own for two years before you got here. So don't get bossy with me."

Jake hid a scowl. If he said he wasn't "getting bossy" she'd argue that he was. And if he admitted to being bossy for a good reason, he'd end up telling her it wasn't safe for her to be here—with the same result. He looked around—saw a smoke detector above the small galley area and another one above the door to the game room. The best he could do was change the subject. "When's your birthday?"

"Next Wednesday. Why?"

"Because I'd like to make dinner for you."

"Wrong. You want to hover."

He smiled. "Okay, I want to hover. But I also like to make a mess in the kitchen occasionally, and I rarely do that for myself. Do you like lasagna? I'm not a great cook, but my mom's Italian so there was never a shortage of red sauce at our house." He waited for her to say something. When she didn't, he tried to sweeten the pot. "I make it with Italian sausage and fresh tomatoes. It's pretty good."

She smiled finally. "Okay. Thank you. I'd like that."

No time like the present to push a little harder for safety. "Now can I say something else without making you mad?"

She rested her hand on the doorknob. "Depends on what it is."

"If you're intent on sleeping here—living here—I want you to keep Maggie for a while." He nearly fell over when she didn't give him an argument.

"Thank you. I will. Whether you believe this or not, I do have enough sense to be afraid." She took her hand off the knob for a moment. "Can I say something to you now? And will you give it some thought before you tell me it's not plausible?"

Jake nodded. "Go ahead."

"I honestly can't think of anyone who might want to hurt me—and I've given it a lot of consideration. So I keep thinking that the man who set the fire might not have meant to kill me. Maybe he counted on my having smoke and heat detectors—like nearly everyone else in the country."

"And if you're right, that means you're safe, and you're worrying for nothing."

"Yes."

Jake stepped closer to her and opened the door, felt the cool night air hit his face. Now *he* was worried. Make that *more* worried. "Don't get complacent," he said, ushering her out. "That's not a good idea."

Twenty minutes later, Jake followed Rachel's Explorer up the slight knoll to the Blackberry, then pulled in beside her to say good-night. She'd insisted that she didn't need an escort, so he told her he wouldn't follow her—then did. He couldn't help himself. Maybe she was entertaining the idea that she might not be at risk, but he wasn't letting his guard down until Perris or the state guys arrested somebody.

Shutting off her headlights, Rachel walked around her car to his open window. At the well-lit side entrance, a tall, slender woman wearing a floppy hat was tapping her code into the keypad outside. Now that Jenna was open for business again, her security system was constantly on for the safety of her guests. The heavy wood-and-etched glass front door was locked up tight.

"I thought you weren't going to follow me," Rachel said, failing to hide the amusement in her voice.

Crickets chirped nearby, and from somewhere down the street, a woman called hollowly to someone named Helen and said to travel safely. Jake got out of his truck. "I didn't. Turns out we were both headed for the same place."

"Liar."

"No, liars are bad people. I'm more of a fibber because I had your best interests at heart." Or maybe it was *his* best interests he was more concerned about tonight. The moon was high, the night air felt good, and he didn't want to go home. Maggie didn't kiss the way Rachel did. And in the part of his mind that insisted on total honesty—the part that missed and craved human touch—he admitted that he'd been thinking all night about kissing her. Jake looked into her eyes and saw her strength and vulnerability, saw her hurt and her resilience, saw her soft, soft lips.

"You were saying?" she prompted with a little hitch in her voice.

Yes, he was certain he'd said something, but right now, he couldn't remember what it was. He let a breath out slowly and wondered about that little break in her voice and the fact that she didn't step back from him. Was that a signal? Did David Patterson's wife want him to kiss her again? And would she kiss him back?

Only one way to find out, that voice in his head said.

Jake agreed.

Easing away from the truck's door, he slid his hand into the soft hair at her nape, then nudged her forward and lowered his mouth to hers. He tasted her sweetness and her warmth, and for several long moments, their lips clung, both of them savoring the contact, savoring the closeness. Until a car's headlights lit their faces and Rachel sprang back. Jake squinted into the high beams, wondering why the idiot driver behind the wheel didn't dim his lights. Then the driver didn't just dim them, she parked her sleek black Corvette and got out, her long blond hair shining in the glow of the lamplights.

Unbelievable, he thought, feeling a nerve work in his jaw. First she shows up in Charity without an invitation, now this. "What are you doing here, Heather?"

Rachel took another step away from him, her retreat feeling a lot more distant than it was.

His ex smiled brightly. "I was coming back from your place when I saw all the lights on at the inn and decided to ask Ms. Harper to put me on a waiting list. I'm just not happy at the travel lodge." She rolled her eyes. "You saw what the room looked like. Anyway, you weren't home, so I looked around and found Maggie in her pen. I loved her up for a while. She hasn't forgotten me."

Who could? Custer could forget the Little Big Horn before he forgot Heather. And which one of his "friends" thought giving her his address was a good idea? Lowering his voice, he turned to Rachel.

"I'll see you inside?"

"No," she replied demurely. "It's late. We can talk tomorrow. Good night, Jake."

Before he could reply and Rachel could get away, Heather strode forward to clasp her hand, thin bracelets tinkling at the edge of her snug, long-sleeved black knit top. "Apparently Jake doesn't want to introduce us," she said with a smile, "so I'll do it. It's nice to meet you. I'm Heather. Jake and I were engaged for a while."

"And then we weren't," Jake cut in.

Softening her voice, Heather looked up at him. "I need to talk to you. I know you're still angry, but it's important. Is there somewhere we can go? You'll want to hear what I have to say."

He seriously doubted that, but Rachel was already striding toward that side entrance, and he didn't want to make her any more uncomfortable by calling her back. "Just spit it out," he said. "What do you want to tell me?"

* * *

Rachel stood in the front doorway peering through the etched glass, far enough away that she couldn't be seen from the parking lot. She couldn't breathe. Heather Quinn was the most strikingly beautiful woman she'd ever seen, with skin like honey and luminous blond hair that had probably never seen a split end. Her clingy black knit top and snug, dark jeans were obviously expensive—as were her gold bracelets and hoop earrings. Rachel swallowed, acutely aware of her lackluster yellow T-shirt, department store jeans and the no-fuss shag her hairstylist had assured her was trendy-chic.

She released a ragged sigh. Outside, the Jake-and-Heather drama was unfolding under the lights, with Heather gradually moving closer to him. She reached up to touch his face.

Rachel glanced away, feeling like a voyeur, feeling like a fool. Only minutes ago, he'd kissed her, and she'd kissed him back, wanting it to last until the sun rose. And now… Slowly, she hazarded another look through the glass.

Both vehicles were leaving the driveway, their red brake lights glowing as they paused at the bottom of the incline. Two sets of left-turn signals flashed. Then Jake followed Heather's Corvette toward the travel lodge… and Rachel's heart sank.

EIGHT

Rachel stepped outside the Blackberry at six-twenty the next morning, thoroughly unsettled, her mind running rampant with images of Heather and Jake. Was he with her now? Sharing a bagel? Taking Maggie for a walk on the country road she and Jake usually walked? Talking things through and finding their way back to each other?

A lump rose in her throat, and for what had to be the fortieth time, she told herself that what he did was his own business. Still, he deserved better than a woman who'd betrayed his trust and left him so jaded that he'd completely closed himself off to future relationships.

She would have climbed inside her Explorer and driven straight out of the driveway if he hadn't called to her from two vehicles away.

Forcing a smile, she turned around and watched him walk toward her. He wore jeans and a black T-shirt that hugged his shoulders—and he didn't appear to be in a good mood.

"Good morning," she said.

"Good morning," he repeated. "I'm sorry about last night."

Which part? she wanted to ask. Their kiss? Heather's

arrival? Or what happened after he and Heather left the Blackberry together? "No problem," she replied, keeping things light as she opened her car door. She tossed her purse and the bag of pastries Jenna had given her on the passenger's seat, then stood beside the car's open doorway. "Heather's very beautiful."

"Heather's a lot of things," he said, then changed the subject. "I figured you'd be heading to the campground early with Tim and his crew coming back today. But I'd hoped you'd be leaving with someone."

"Jenna has guests," she said, sorting through her key ring. "She can't leave whenever she feels like it."

He didn't say anything for a long moment, then he sighed. "You're annoyed with me."

"No," she said quickly lifting her gaze. Apparently her acting skills needed work. "No, I'm not." She was just concerned that he was about to make a mistake he'd regret for the rest of his life. At least that's what she told herself. But she could hardly share that with him because—

Yes, I know, a voice weary of repetition whispered. *What Jake does is Jake's business.*

"All right, if you're not annoyed, then why are you being so distant?"

Rachel felt the tightness in her chest ease a little with the honest concern she saw in his dark eyes. "I'm sorry. I don't mean to be. I'm just in a hurry to get to the campground to see how things went last night. And I'm tired. I'm still not sleeping well."

"Considering everything you're dealing with, that's no surprise."

And now she could add Jake's emotional well-being to the list.

He held her car door open and nodded for her to get inside. "Hop in. I'll follow you."

"You don't have to. It's broad daylight. No one's going to bother me."

"Probably not, but humor me."

"What about your work?"

"If someone calls while I'm out, the number for the regional office is on my machine. They'll contact me. Today I just need to be available."

Interesting word, Rachel thought, that lump back in her throat as she started her car and backed out of her parking space. *Was* he available? And what was Heather doing this morning while Jake played bodyguard? She wasn't the type to sit alone in her room. She was too confident, too vibrant, and if Rachel's intuition was working even a little bit…too determined to get Jake back.

When they got to the campground, Wes Atkins was pulling away in his SUV, while Joe Reston watched from cabin three's small porch. Joe had a foam cup of coffee in his hand, courtesy of the small coffeemaker and condiments Rachel had put in the cabin yesterday. He walked out to meet them as she and Jake left their respective vehicles.

"Wes said the night went smoothly—no problems to report."

"Thank heaven," Rachel said. "You're his replacement?"

"Yeah. Roy's kid had an orthodontist appointment this morning, so he'll take over at three. We really appreciate your letting us set our own hours."

He glanced at Jake, and Rachel could see there was

no love lost there. "You come up with a way to keep the elk out of my hay field yet?"

Jake didn't reply. There was no way to keep eight-hundred-pound elk out of farmers' open fields and orchards. They roamed where they pleased.

Reston nodded. "That's what I thought." He shifted his attention back to Rachel. "I'll just finish my coffee, gas up the golf cart and take a ride. Anything else you'd like me to do? Feels like I'm getting paid for sightseeing."

"No, just be a presence. But thanks for offering." The man had a problem with fidelity, but he wasn't afraid of work. "See you later," she said as he waved and ambled toward the golf cart.

She turned to Jake and mustered a smile. "Well, Joe's here, so if there's something you need to do—"

His brow furrowed. "I've already told you I'm not busy. Do you want me to leave?"

"I want you to do what you need to do," she said honestly—whether that was work for the commission, or spending time with Heather.

"Rachel, my laptop's in my truck, my paperwork for the week is nearly finished and your campground has Wi-Fi if I need to send it. But it's not important that I do it right this minute. Now what can I do to lighten your load?"

They turned as engine and heavy equipment sounds carried to them from the highway. A moment later, brawny Tim Decker and his crew came down the driveway rumbling and clanking their way toward the construction site.

Tim waved to her from the long flatbed truck

carrying the bulldozer, and she waved back, praying that nothing would stand in the way of their putting in a full day's work. The clock was ticking toward opening day.

She turned back to Jake. "What can you do to lighten my load?" Smiling again, she handed the pastry bag to him. "You can belly up to my lunch counter while I make coffee to go with these. They're cranberry-apple muffins. Jenna insisted that I take a dozen to share with the men, and you just happen to be a man." A tall, ruggedly good-looking man who'd become far too important to her.

They were enjoying a second cup of coffee when the roar of construction machinery ceased and a bevy of excited shouts shattered the morning calm. Exchanging a startled look, they leaped from their stools and pushed through the screen door.

Please, Rachel prayed as they raced down the driveway to the trampled grass near the site. *Please don't let anyone be hurt.* She could see Tim now, standing silently with his men, their expressions dour.

Tim's uneasy gaze met hers as they approached, and he exhaled raggedly. "Sorry, Rachel. Looks like we're shut down again." Then he stepped back to give her a clear view of the chewed-up ground and sod...and the hairs at the back of Rachel's neck stood on end.

Directly in front of the dozer blade was a scattered human skeleton, its skull lolling at a sickening angle some distance from the body. Rachel drew a steadying breath. There appeared to be a bullet hole above the left eye socket.

"Dear God," Rachel whispered, a chill running through her.

Jake spoke quietly from behind her. "Better call Perris. I think we know what your prowler was looking for now."

Jake hung back several yards while Chief Lon Perris stood at the edge of the crime scene conferring with two state police officers. Nearby, new-hire, Patrolman Call Drago, took photographs and the county coroner unzipped a body bag. There'd been no wallet, I.D. or jewelry with the remains, but pieces of ragged clothing had been recovered along with a plastic beer chip from a tavern in the next county. Luckily, the dental work seemed to be in good-enough shape to quickly identify the victim if he was local. Charity had only two dentists. Jake had overheard the coroner say he suspected that the body had been in the ground for four or five years, but that was only his best guess.

Perris said something to the staties, then walked over to where Jake and Rachel stood. "Let's go somewhere and talk, shall we, Mrs. Patterson?" He glanced up at the sky. "Preferably out of the sun."

"Of course," she replied. She sent Jake an entreating look. "Coming with me?"

He nodded. You bet he was. He'd been involved since the prowler incident nine days ago. He wasn't backing away now.

Minutes later, he eased back against the nearby pop machine while Perris took a seat on a stool at the camp store's counter and Rachel lowered herself to the one beside him. She slid their coffee cups aside.

Perris pulled out a pen and notebook. "Okay, Mrs. Patterson. It's Q and A time again. Any guesses as to the vic's identity?"

She shook her head. "None at all."

"No campers went missing in the past five years?"

"I don't do a head count when they check out, but no one ever mentioned a missing friend or relative."

"And how long have you owned the campground?"

"It was my late-husband's when we married six years ago," she said. "But the property where the bones were found wasn't mine until recently."

Perris raised a black eyebrow. "It wasn't?"

"No, I inherited it from an elderly man who passed away last year. I'd asked him several times if I could buy it because Willard—Mr. Trehern—had no plan to use it. By itself, it was too narrow to build on. But it bordered my land and was big enough for a putt-putt golf course."

"Trehern just left it to you? There was no provision in the will for payment to be made to his next of kin?"

Rachel shook her head. "I had no idea he'd given it to me until Jillian came by after the will had been read and handed me the deed."

Perris scribbled another note in his book. "Does this Jillian have a last name?"

"Donner," Rachel replied, resisting the urge to say that everyone had a last name. "Will Trehern was her uncle. I don't think he had any other relatives. None that I know of anyway."

"Then she got the rest of Trehern's estate?"

"I believe so."

The chief took a minute to think. "Any chance she didn't like sharing her inheritance?"

Jake watched Rachel's face line. "What do you mean?"

"I mean, was there any reluctance on her part when she gave you the deed?"

Apparently she didn't like Perris's tone because she answered firmly, "Absolutely not. Jillian was glad I'd be using the land to make kids happy. She and her husband never had children."

Perris folded his notebook and tucked it into his shirt pocket. "Okay. Hopefully we'll get a hit on the vic's clothing and dental work. In the meantime, no one crosses the yellow-tape line until we've finished examining the surrounding woods and area."

Rachel sent Jake a brief, startled look. "For...more bodies?" she asked.

"Stranger things have happened," Perris replied, then stood. "But basically, we're still looking for a bullet." He sent her an odd look before he walked to the screen door. Then as if he'd read Jake's uneasy thoughts, he spoke again. "Mrs. Patterson, if the man you saw last week was here to dig up those bones before the heavy equipment moved in, and he thinks you recognized him—or saw something that would lead us to him—you could be in a world of trouble. I understand you've hired a few men for security purposes. That's a step in the right direction. But it might be better if you left the area for a while."

When Perris had gone—presumably to join the PSP officers—Jake straightened from the pop machine and walked to Rachel. He didn't like the tight feeling in his chest. "Are you okay?"

She blew out a shaky breath. "Yes."

He didn't believe her for an instant. She'd mentioned having a target on her back after the arson report, but there'd been a trace of flippancy in her voice. Now the reality of her situation had been driven home.

"The idea of multiple bodies buried on my land gives me chills, but I'm okay." Her words and breathing were coming too fast. "What a tragic end to a life. He had to have been someone's son or father or uncle or brother, but I never read or heard about anyone in the area disappearing. Shouldn't someone have missed him?"

"Maybe he wasn't from the area," Jake said.

Rachel scooped up their cups, then cried out as one of them crashed to the floor. Jake took the other mug from her and set it on the counter. Her hands were shaking. "Sit down for a minute," he said. "Take some time. The chief just laid a lot on you."

"No, no," she blurted, quickly stooping to pick up the pieces. "I did it. I need to clean it up."

He eased Rachel to her feet—took the chunky pieces of stoneware from her and put it them on the counter, too. There were no tears. But the fear in her eyes nearly brought him to his knees. Unable to stop himself, he gathered her close, inhaled the citrus fragrance of her hair, liked too much the feel of her in his arms.

"Just breathe," he murmured. "Nothing's going to happen to you while Maggie and I are around. But the chief's right. Leaving the area for a while is a very good idea."

The screen door swung open with a long testy creak, and a woman spoke. "Rachel, why are there police vehicles parked—"

Rachel sprang back, her cheeks flushing guiltily. "Clarissa, hello."

Jake watched her cross the floor to a puzzled-looking woman who appeared to be in her sixties. The woman's height and hair were both short—the latter, curly and dyed a weird burgundy shade. The jeans and long green shirt she wore with her flat sandals should have made her appear even shorter, but for some reason, didn't. Maybe because of the strength he saw in her gray eyes.

Frowning, she hugged Rachel and kissed her cheek. "I know you said when you phoned that you didn't need anything, but Mamie Jackson called last night to tell me that the fire was arson. I had to come." She released her hold on Rachel, then sent him a frosty, what's-going-on-here? stare.

Rachel handled the introductions with grace. "Clarissa, this is my neighbor, Jake Campbell. He bought the Britmeyers' log cabin down the road when he moved here. Jake, Clarissa Patterson. David's mother."

For a second, Jake froze in place. Then he smiled and shook the woman's outstretched hand. Now he understood Rachel's uneasy reaction. Obviously, he wouldn't be sticking around now, but he *would* be staying close. "Nice to meet you, Mrs. Patterson."

"Likewise, Mr. Campbell," she replied, assessing him. She glanced between Jake and Rachel. "You moved here recently?"

"Yes, six months ago. I'm the new wildlife conservation officer. Game warden, if you're more familiar with that term."

"I am. Are you enjoying the area, Mr. Campbell?"

Was there a hidden question there? Was she also asking if he was enjoying her son's widow? There was still no way to answer except honestly. "I like it a lot. It's similar to my old stomping grounds, although the mountains here are steeper. I've made some good friends."

He glanced at Rachel who was still trying to hide her awkwardness. "I'll get out of here so you can catch Mrs. Patterson up on the news before it hits the papers. You might want to call your parents, too."

He heard Clarissa's nervous "What's happened?" but he kept his eyes on Rachel.

"I'm not sure that's a good idea," Rachel replied.

"It would be better coming from you than a friend who still lives here. You know how stories get twisted around."

She nodded. "You're right. Thanks for following me down here this morning."

"Anytime," he replied. He battled with decorum for a moment, then said what he needed to say. If Mrs. Patterson objected...well, she'd just have to object. "I'll stop by again in a little while. Call if you need me. I'll be home." Then he pushed through the screen door and crossed the driveway to his truck. He was climbing into the cab when he heard Clarissa Patterson's shocked voice.

"They uncovered a body? Oh, dear God, Rachel, I wish David were here."

There was no other way for her to respond, but Jake still felt a sharp twinge when Rachel said, "So do I."

Rachel was still feeling uneasy when Clarissa—not Jake—followed her back to the Blackberry, then left to visit with Mamie Jackson before returning home to Johnstown. Unlike Rachel's parents, the Pattersons hadn't made their home in Charity—had always lived in the southern part of the state. But when David followed his heart to the woods, they'd visited their son often and formed friendships here.

Jenna was in the combination sitting room–library polishing cherrywood tables to a gleaming patina when Rachel walked in. Even dressed casually in plum-colored knit pants and a boat-necked, creamy, three-quarter-sleeve tunic, her beautiful friend looked *Vogue* chic. Jenna wore tunics and long sweaters often, but not to hide a tummy or thick waistline. Tunics didn't ride up. Tunics didn't reveal scars.

When Rachel had finished blurting out the day's happenings, Jenna put down her soft cloth and beeswax polish and steered Rachel to a faux-antique sofa. She sat down beside her. "A body," she said on a stunned breath.

"Yes. Clarissa offered to stay in Charity for a while. Her husband passed away before David died, so she's able to come and go when she wants. But I told her there was no need—that I was staying with you and friends were taking good care of me." She sent Jenna a bleak look. "She asked if Jake was one of them."

"He was there when she arrived?"

She nodded. "And he came back later to see how I was doing. Eventually she asked if we were dating. I think she felt better when I told her he'd probably be reconciling with his ex."

Jenna looked surprised. "You're not serious."

"I don't know. Jake isn't talking about her."

"Then why would you say that he was recon—?"

"Because he was holding me when she walked in, and I felt guilty." Rachel hurried to clarify. "Not the romantic kind of holding. I was upset, and he was just trying to make me feel better—the way any friend would."

"I think he's more than a friend," Jenna said quietly,

then left it at that and changed the subject. She looked at Rachel intently. "You said Perris and Jake both think you should leave for a while and let your staff handle the campground opening."

"Yes, but I can't. There's still a lot of work to do, and I don't feel comfortable leaving it in inexperienced hands. The kids I hire are only there to watch the store, cut the grass and see that trash is collected. The only thing I can do is give it all to God. My life—"

"Your fears?"

That was a tall order. "As much as I can."

Now fear clouded Jenna's eyes. "Rachel, I believe that God watches over us, too. He gives us the grace we need to get through difficult times. But you need to do more than put this in His hands. There are people in this world who are so…so malevolent, so inherently evil that they won't stop until they accomplish their goals. The man who burned your home could try to hurt you again."

Gooseflesh covered Rachel's arms, but she still tried to look at things logically. "Maybe not. The campground will be crawling with police and heaven knows who else for the next day or two, so I'd think he'd want to keep a low profile at this point—hope that the police lab won't link any evidence they find to him. He might even run if he lives nearby." She sent her friend a tentative look. "Jen, whoever did this is dangerous. But he's not Courtland Dane."

Jenna curved a hand over her stomach. It was an automatic gesture that Rachel had seen many times. "I realize that. But I'm living proof that when a man feels the need to kill, he acts without thinking things through rationally." She paused. "I have a proposition for you."

"What kind of proposition?"

"I want you to stay with me until Perris has someone in custody." Rachel started to object, but Jenna went on. "All right, you can pay me the going rate, but please… don't move into your camp store. I have an excellent security system and the police are nearby. You'll be safe here."

To Rachel's relief, the phone rang, and Jenna left the room to answer it. She didn't want her friend to worry but she couldn't accept her offer, even though her stomach still shook and her fear was nearly indescribable. She knew she'd be jumping at shadows every time she heard an unfamiliar noise. But with Maggie at her side, Jake checking on her and constant security on the grounds, she should be okay.

Shouldn't she?

Jenna reentered the room carrying a cordless handset, her expression still full of concern. She handed Rachel the phone. "It's Margo calling from Kentucky. She wanted an update on the arson. You should tell her what you just told me."

Rachel accepted the phone, then repeated the day's events to her other best friend. When they'd talked at length, with Margo apologizing profusely for not being able to be with her, Rachel thanked her, said a warm goodbye and broke the connection.

Jenna had given her some space while she spoke on the phone. Now she walked slowly back to the sofa they'd been sharing and sat down. Something was on her mind.

"What?" Rachel asked.

"I was just thinking about the three of us—the way our lives have gone. What is it about us that invites trouble? Margo was threatened by a serial killer, I was… hurt. And now you're dealing with this horror."

Rachel shook her head. She had no answers. In His mercy, God had seen that Margo and Jenna survived. She could only hope that He would watch over her, as well.

"I can't stay here indefinitely, Jen," she said, finally addressing Jenna's offer. "I have to take control of my life. This—" She drew a breath, felt prickles of fear again. "This thug who wants to hurt me could be a very patient man. I can't hide out forever. I'm moving back to the campground tomorrow."

The night-light shone dimly in the near dark of Rachel's upstairs room, and from outside a balmy breeze floated through the window, billowing the sheer curtains beneath the drapes. Unlike the first-floor windows, the Blackberry's second-floor panes were free from the added mesh barriers Jenna had installed when she bought the B & B from her great-aunt.

Rachel got out of bed, walked around her packed bag, then crossed to the window. She looked out on the sleeping town. Fear could be a debilitating thing, but she didn't want to be so afraid to die that she was afraid to live. She couldn't do that. No matter how concerned her mother had been on the phone tonight. Then again, she hadn't given her mom the entire story. She'd told her about the fire, skipped the part about arson, then, only later, brought up the body that had been uncovered. She'd prayed tonight that no one from Charity would call and fill in the blanks before she had a chance to. No parent needed to hear that her only child could be in mortal danger over the telephone. That news had to come face-to-face.

"What do you think, God?" she asked quietly. "Am I being an idiot for staying when so many people want me to leave?"

The extension in her room rang, and she had to smile a little, wondering if she was about to get His answer firsthand. Crossing to the Queen Anne nightstand, she picked up the phone. The alarm clock beside it said it was nine-forty-three.

It wasn't God. It was Jake.

His deep voice burred against her ear. "I hope it's not too late to call."

"No, I was awake. Thinking."

"Again—not surprised." He paused, seeming to search for conversation. "The staties were at your putt-putt site for a long time tonight."

"Are they really looking for more bodies?"

"I don't know. They didn't bring in dogs or radar. I think they were just looking for areas that might have been disturbed recently. But I didn't call to talk about forensics."

Rachel waited through his pause.

"I hope I didn't make things too uncomfortable for you today when your mother-in-law was there. I think she got the wrong idea about us."

If she had an ounce of courage in her body, she'd tell him that Clarissa had gotten the *right* idea. She'd seen the chemistry between them, otherwise she wouldn't have asked if they were dating. "Clarissa drove back to Johnstown. She wanted to stay, but I told her I'd be okay."

"Did you call your parents?"

"Yes, earlier this evening, then again a little while ago."

"And?"

Rachel lowered herself to the bed. "I'm going to squeeze in a trip to Virginia. I didn't tell my mom everything. I need to let her know about the bad stuff in person."

"Good. When are you leaving?"

"As soon as the sun comes up. I told Jenna that I was moving back to the campground tomorrow, but now...I have to take care of my family first."

"Stay there," he said. "Stay in Williamsburg until this is resolved."

"I can't."

He expelled a weary blast of air. "Okay. But if you don't mind, I'd like to make a few changes at your camp store if you're determined to live there."

"What kind of changes?"

"Nothing you'll object to. Just be careful on the roads and call me when you get to your parents' home."

"I will," she replied.

"Good night, then."

"Good night. I'll see you in a few days."

Rachel hung up, then slipped beneath the covers again, wondering what he'd be doing while she was away. He and his protective streak would get a well-deserved break with her out of the picture. And that would free him up to do other things. See other people.

She sent a tentative glance at the phone, hesitated, then reached over to click on the antique lamp on the nightstand and pull the phone book from the drawer. After searching the yellow pages for hotel and motel listings, she eased back against her stacked pillows to stare at the ad for the Tall Spruce Travel Lodge. They had all the fancy extras. Air-conditioned units, satellite TV, Wi-Fi, a workout room, pool and spa and a free hot breakfast. Committing the number to memory, she returned the phone book to the drawer.

Eventually, she shook her head, told herself to grow up and turned off the lamp. She was a mature adult. She wasn't a jealous teenager who longed to see if the competition was still in town.

That emotional ache in Rachel's chest came back, and she rolled over and closed her eyes. Sleep didn't come.

She knew about love. It lasted. It lived in the heart and moved through the veins like a warm elixir. But she didn't believe that love automatically ended with betrayal, no matter how painful the breakup. People continued to hurt because they continued to love.

She couldn't imagine Jake feeling any differently.

Her parents' Williamsburg home was a white colonial two-story with white columns and black trim, and it was situated in a lovely neighborhood where huge azalea and rhododendron bushes were in full bloom. Her pretty mom was through the front door and down the steps to greet her as soon as Rachel drove in. Annie Morgan's smile and outstretched arms looked so warm and welcoming that Rachel couldn't wait to fill them.

"I'm so sorry about the house," her mom murmured, tears in her eyes now. "Are you okay at Jenna's?"

"No, I'm better than okay." Rachel stepped back to admire her mother. Lord willing, this was how she'd look at sixty. Annie Foster Morgan's sable hair was sprinkled lightly with gray now, and her green eyes were a shade lighter than Rachel's. But their resemblance was striking. The only thing Rachel hadn't inherited from her mom was her classic sense of style. Today she wore pale green linen trousers and a darker green three-quarter-sleeve sweater with tiny roses circling the scooped neckline.

"You're sure?" Annie said.

"I'm sure. Jenna's been terrific. Everyone has. This morning before I left, Reverend Landers's wife came by to see if there was anything more the church could do for me. I have good friends, Mom."

"Thank God for that." Slipping an arm around Rachel's waist, she walked her toward the house, a slight sadness in her smile. "Leave your bags in the car for now, okay? Your dad's anxious to talk to you. He'll feel better seeing for himself that you weren't hurt."

Rachel nodded. The last thing in the world she wanted to do was make her dad anxious. "He has nothing to worry about," she replied in as light a tone as she could muster. "Fires happen, and people rebuild. I'm not jumping for joy over it, but I'm tough—like you." She gave her mom another big hug. "Now let's go inside so I can give Dad one of these, too."

They were almost to the door when the cell phone in the pocket of Rachel's borrowed pink jacket chimed out a melody, and excusing herself, she checked the number. A breathy feeling of expectation filled her chest.

"Jake, hi," she said, smiling.

His voice was low and worried. "Hi. I thought you were going to call when you got to Williamsburg."

"I was and I will. But I just got here. I haven't even had time to say hello to my dad or unpack yet." Her mother sent her a smile and a raised eyebrow, and Rachel smiled back. "Let me call you back in a little while. I need to catch up with my folks first."

"I hope it goes well."

"Me, too. Keep your fingers crossed." Then she dropped her voice, said, "Talk to you soon" and slipped the phone back in her pocket.

"That was your neighbor? The game protector who lives down the road from you?"

Rachel laughed. "Mom, I know that look, and it's not what you think. He just called to make sure I got here safely."

"But he was concerned about you?"

"Maybe a little," she replied, trying not to put too much importance on the call—for both of their sakes. "Why?"

Annie Morgan released a lung-clearing sigh and smiled. "No reason, except that I think...I think I'm less worried about you now."

NINE

Tired from driving straight through from Williamsburg, Rachel clicked on her left-turn signal and turned down the long driveway into her campground. She'd left her parents' home early enough to beat most of the traffic, but she'd gotten tied up on I-64 anyway. Now dusk was approaching, and the descending sun streaked the sky with golden pinks and purples. Still, she felt relatively safe, despite returning this late. She'd called Jenna with her ETA a while ago, and one of the guys would be patrolling the grounds. She'd just check out the campground, grab a cold drink, then head to town.

The first things she noticed when her camp store came into view were Jake's truck parked beside the utility barn, and Maggie scouting the tall ferns and undergrowth down near the second camping loop. Then she saw Jake walking up from the wreckage that had been her home. As she'd come to expect now, Rachel felt a warm glow of attraction. He'd been out running again. His loose-fitting gray tank top and denim cutoffs showcased a lot of tan and a well-toned physique. She'd missed him these past two days.

That warm glow faded when she spotted her door. Quickly parking beside the store, she got out and took another look. Twenty yards away, Jake was closing the distance between them.

"Welcome back," he called. Taking a white hand towel from his back pocket, he wiped his face. Damp brown hair in need of a trim clung to his forehead.

"Thanks. It's good to be back. Where's my door?"

"Right where it should be. Hanging on its hinges."

"My *wooden* door," she returned, fairly certain he didn't need the clarification. "The door with the new glass pane."

He was beside her now, a bit of exertion still coloring his voice. "Gone, but not forgotten apparently. You'll like the steel door better. I know I will. It didn't take much effort on your part to smash out the glass and get inside the night of the fire. Someone else could do the same."

Flicking him a warning glance, she opened the screen door, then her new windowless door and stepped inside. "You can't do things like this."

"I didn't." He followed her in. "Keys are on the counter."

"Then who did?" She couldn't imagine Clarissa arranging it. And how had Joe Reston and the Atkins brothers failed to notice someone replacing a door? Everyone had her cell phone number, and they'd promised to use it if anything out of the ordinary happened.

"Okay," Jake said, dropping to a stool. "I bought the door, but Ben Caruthers donated the locks and hardware, and suggested a local carpenter to install it. Beau Travis. There was no charge. Travis said you knew each other from church."

Rachel winced. "We do, but we're not close. For that matter, neither are Ben and I." Slipping behind the lunch counter, she took two Pepsis from her refrigerator, then slid one across the bar to Jake. "I'll write you a check. Ben and Beau, too."

"I won't cash it."

"Then I'll find another way to repay you."

"Rachel," he said, sighing. "Why can't you just—?"

"Because I'm not comfortable with charity when I'm the recipient. When you said you wanted to make a few changes, I half expected you to hang another motion light and post a Protected by Smith & Wesson sign out front. A steel door is excessive. It's too much and it's too expensive."

"Then I guess it's best that I didn't buy the travel trailer." He popped the tab on his soda.

Rachel stared in numb disbelief. "You're kidding."

"No. I considered it, but I was afraid you'd get ticked off."

"You were right." Shaking her head, she marched out to her car, grabbed her pen and checkbook from the locked glove box and returned to sit beside him. "How much for the door?"

"I don't know. I don't have a receipt."

"Look," she said, frustrated now, "I might have to rely on my friends for a sympathetic ear or a shoulder to cry on occasionally. But so much has happened that I have no control over, that I need to handle the things I can. My parents, Clarissa, you, Ben and half the town think I'm about to curl into a ball and roll away. That's not going to happen. Now, how much?"

Finally seeming to understand, Jake nodded apologetically. "I'm sorry. I haven't been billed yet, but I'll give you the invoice when it comes in." He hesitated.

"And if you think you absolutely have to, you can add a few bucks for—"

A long, high-pitched beep sounded, and Rachel stood quickly to look around. "What was that?"

Jake sent her another rueful look. "I was getting to that. A vehicle just broke the beam of the electronic sensor near the top of your driveway. You're getting company."

Rachel didn't know whether to thank him for caring or throw him out. David had always sheltered her, and after his passing, she'd come to value her independence. She didn't want anyone making decisions that affected her life without her knowledge—no matter what their motives were.

"I'll need the bill for that, too," she said, heading for the screen door to watch for her "company."

"You're angry," Jake said.

She turned back to him. "No. The alarm was a good idea. Thank you. It'll be great while I'm here alone, but when my guests start coming in, it'll have to be disabled."

"That won't be a problem. I'll take care of it."

"Good."

Tires crunched over limestone chips as a police cruiser rolled past the screen door and pulled in next to Rachel's Explorer. Pulse quickening, she went out to meet Chief Lon Perris. But as he shut off the engine and exited the vehicle, she experienced a niggling feeling of apprehension. His lean, pockmarked features were set in stone, and there was a coolness in his black eyes that told her trouble was on the way.

"Good evening, Mrs. Patterson."

"Good evening," she repeated, showing him inside,

then motioning him to a stool near Jake. When Perris chose to remain standing, Rachel did the same. Jake rose, too.

"How was your trip?" he asked. "I looked for you at the bed and breakfast, but Ms. Harper told me you'd planned to stop here on your way back from Virginia."

"It was very nice, thank you. But you didn't drive down here to ask about my visit."

"No, I didn't." He gave Jake a once-over, then shifted his gaze back to Rachel. "I thought I should tell you in person that we've ID'd the victim. Dental records confirmed that he was the former owner of the local lumber mill."

Stunned, she spoke in a hushed voice. "Bryce? Bryce Donner?"

Jake looked at her. "You knew him?"

"As a matter of fact, she did," Perris said before Rachel could speak. "Mrs. Patterson and the deceased were what some people used to call 'an item.' Maybe they still do. She and Mr. Donner were high school steadies and had a nearly two-year relationship after that before she broke it off." He paused. "Or have I been misinformed?"

Rachel shook her head, still trying to comprehend how Bryce could be those skeletal remains. He'd made enemies while he was alive, but did anyone deserve such a horrifying death and burial? "We...we dated sporadically. But that was years ago. How did you—"

"—know about it?" he asked. "You've lived here your whole life. You should know that the locals have long memories. I'm sorry for your loss."

He was sorry for *her* loss? What was going on here?

"And now," Perris said, with a pointed glance at Jake. "Maybe it would be best if we finished speaking about this privately."

Rachel hid her growing concern. "No. Jake can hear anything you have to say to me."

"Fine. Then I understand your late-husband used to work for Mr. Donner—and that Donner was a guest at your wedding down here in the woods."

Rachel's pulse accelerated. Suddenly she knew where this was going. "David changed jobs after our marriage."

"Which is certainly understandable," Perris returned coolly. "I'd have done the same if Donner had gotten all liquored up and tried to do more than kiss my bride. Except, your husband didn't quit, did he? He was fired."

Jake felt every hair on his head prickle, and he slid a cautious look at Rachel. She'd gone pale. His protective instincts kicked in. "Mind if I ask what any of this has to do with your investigation, Chief?" But he knew. Oh, yeah. He knew.

"Your screams brought Patterson and several witnesses running," Perris went on, ignoring Jake's question. "And in short order, Mr. Donner had a broken nose and cheekbone, and your brand-new husband was out of a job." He gave her a moment to digest that. "Now I'd like to know how deeply your hatred for Mr. Donner went. Yours and your husband's."

How she managed to keep her tone cool and polite was a mystery to Jake.

"Neither of us would have ever taken a life. And if you've been asking around about Bryce, then you know that the number of people he hurt in one way or the other is legion. Also, the coroner said Bryce was in the ground for four or five years—and that fight happened a good year beforehand. Why would David or I wait that long to confront Bryce?"

"I couldn't say. But to paraphrase Shakespeare, some people think revenge is a dish best served cold."

Jake stood, unable to harness his irritation. "You're not making sense. First of all, you should be looking for the man Rachel saw at the construction site. Second, someone just tried to burn her home to the ground with her in it. Third, why would she have the land cleared if she knew about—or was responsible for—those bones being there?"

"Mrs. Patterson was the only one who saw the alleged intruder, and her home was adequately insured. I know that because I checked. As for her developing the land, what better way to allay suspicion from her and her husband?"

Angry tears glistened in Rachel's eyes, and her voice shook. "Are you charging me with something?"

"Not at all. I'm just checking out rumors and doing my job. You're not the only person I've spoken with today."

"In that case," she said, striding to the screen door and opening it wide. "Thank you for stopping by."

"Thank you for your time," he said, either missing her point or choosing to ignore it. "I'll be in touch."

When the screen door had banged shut behind him, Rachel spun from the entry. She was a whirlwind of nerves as she snapped on the light switch beside the door, chasing the evening shadows. "God help me, I want to do something nasty to that man."

Jake felt the same way, and nothing he considered was legal. "He's a jerk. Don't let him get to you."

"How can I not?" Tears splashed over her lower lashes, and she took an impatient swipe at them. "David would never have done anything like that. He was kind and gentle, and he lived the commandments. I doubt he ever completely forgave Bryce, but he would never, ever have taken his life. It's not who he was, and I'm not going to let Perris or anyone else ruin his good name."

Jake fell silent, feelings he didn't want to acknowledge flitting at the edges of his mind. Ten years ago, his grandmother had remarried after being widowed for five years. But before she'd said "I do," she'd come to him, knowing how close he and his granddad had been. She'd told him she would always love his granddad, and she wished with all of her heart that they could still be together. But that wasn't possible. Now she had to be content with her memories...and move on.

Would Rachel ever be able to do that?

Maybe, in time.

But Jake knew about time. It marched on and waited for no one, and eventually ran out. For a man who wanted a home and family someday, time was of the essence.

Slowly, he dropped to a stool again, knowing that as convoluted as his feelings for her were, he'd do what he could to ease her mind. If she wanted to preserve her late-husband's good name, he'd help her. But doing more than that was a mistake.

"Maybe we should look into Donner's murder, too," he said. "Perris is an unknown commodity. If he's lazy about police work—and I'm not saying he is—he could stick your husband with the murder, and he's not here to defend himself."

"David won't have to defend himself," Rachel said testily. "I will." She looked at him. "How do we begin?"

"By asking questions, the same as Perris does."

"Like what?"

"Like who wanted to scratch Donner off his or her Christmas list. You told Perris that the number of people he'd hurt or messed with is legion. We need to talk to them, and to others who knew him." Jake paused. "But for now, you've had a long day. Are you ready to head back to the Blackberry?"

She was.

A half hour later, after they'd wished Wes Atkins good-night and left Maggie in her pen, they entered the Blackberry and threaded their way through the foyer, living room and short hall. They paused outside the formal dining room where Jenna and her great-aunt Molly were discussing the morning menu over tea.

The older woman looked up and smiled.

With a rustle of her floor-length rose taffeta skirt, she swept through the dining room's open French doors to give Rachel a warm hug. Molly Jennings was a tiny white-haired pixie with a feathery cap cut and twinkling blue eyes, who loved dressing in period clothing. She stood nearly five-feet tall in her high button shoes, and Rachel knew the cameo pinned to her long-sleeved, fussy white blouse had been a gift from her late-husband.

"How wonderful to see you, honey," she cooed, eighty-odd years of smiles creasing her pretty features.

"You, too," Rachel said.

"I just wish you were staying with us under different circumstances."

"I guess Jenna told you everything."

"She did," Molly said, releasing her and stepping back. "And I don't like it a bit. Unfortunately, there's nothing an old woman can do about it except give you a bed to sleep in and pray this dreadful business is over soon."

"Prayers and a bed are more than enough," Rachel replied. "Thank you."

Molly and her husband, Charles, had never been blessed with children, but over the years, Molly had loved and claimed many "nieces and nephews." Rachel was one of them. Jenna was special, though. She wasn't merely a blood relative, she was also the closest thing the Jenningses had ever had to a daughter. They had been honored when Jenna's parents had named her after them.

Rachel turned to Jake. "Aunt Molly, I'd like you to meet my friend Jake Campbell. He's been great through all of this."

Molly Jennings's old eyes sparkled. "So I've heard." She extended a hand that was quickly swallowed up in Jake's. "It's very nice to meet you, Mr. Campbell."

"The pleasure's mine, Mrs. Jennings," he said, smiling. "And please call me Jake."

"I'll do that. Now, let's find you a chair because I'm getting a crick in my neck looking up at you."

Jake chuckled. "Thanks, but I should go and let you ladies talk."

"No, you shouldn't," she returned, linking her arm through his and steering him toward the table where she and Jenna had been sipping tea. "I need some time to figure you out."

Rachel and Jenna exchanged smiles, then followed. When the women were seated, Jake lowered himself to a chair.

"Now," Aunt Molly said, propping her elbows on the table and clasping her hands, "what's our illustrious chief of police doing about all of this?"

When Rachel had finished telling her and Jenna about Perris's visit to the campground, Molly pursed her lips. "Makes me wonder if the note Jillian found was actually from Bryce. You know the story, don't you, Rachel?"

Rachel glanced at Jake, then turned to Molly again. "I'm afraid I don't. What note?"

"About five years ago, it was rumored that Bryce was fooling around with a married woman, which may or may not have been the case. He was a hound, that one, so it was easy to believe." She sipped from her china teacup, then returned it to her saucer. "One morning, Jillian came downstairs to find a note and Bryce's wedding band on her kitchen table. Supposedly, there were only two words on the page: 'I'm sorry.' Well, Jillian insisted that they were just going through a rough patch, and Bryce would be back soon. But the rest of the town thought he'd run off with a woman." Aunt Molly harrumphed. "Personally, I thought good riddance to bad rubbish. With him gone, maybe Jillian would finally be able to wear short sleeves again."

Jake cocked his head. "Donner objected to his wife showing her arms?"

"No," Molly replied sternly. "He objected to her showing her bruises."

* * *

Twenty minutes later, Rachel walked Jake to the front door, then followed him out to the wide wraparound porch. The moon was high in the sky, and although the air had cooled, a few stalwart crickets managed a light serenade.

They kept their voices low.

"Interesting story Mrs. Jennings told about Donner's romantic escapades," Jake said. "Sounds like there could be an angry husband or two out there. Or maybe a wife who got tired of being pushed around."

Rachel had to disagree. "You wouldn't say that if you knew Jillian. She's not capable of murder. An angry husband's a possibility, though." She was about to suggest another potential suspect when Jake's solemn features lined in the soft glow of the porch light.

"Did Donner hurt you when you were together?"

She shook her head. "No, my dad would have taken him apart. We knew each other before that element of his personality showed up."

"Good. I'd hoped that wasn't the reason you broke things off." His next words came hesitantly. "You dated him for a long time."

Rachel strolled closer to the steps to gaze at the moon. It was three-quarters full, and wispy clouds drifted across its luminous face. "Too long. I didn't have a brain in my head back then."

"Was it serious?"

She smiled a little. "When you're eighteen, everything's serious." Memories of that time rose in her mind. "I wasn't a very good daughter back then. I gave my parents some sleepless nights."

"Somehow, I can't see that."

"Unfortunately, it's true. I bailed out on college because Bryce said it was a waste of my time and my parents' money. I'd never have to work, he said, because sooner or later the lumber mill would be his. He was a cute, rich, spoiled only child, and I had stars in my eyes."

Jake ambled to the edge of the porch to join her. "Sounds like you and Donner talked about marriage."

She nodded. "Only in the way kids do. It took me two years, but I wised up, got my accounting degree and found a job."

"And you fell in love with David."

"Yes. He was everything Bryce wasn't—solid and unselfish. That's why I can't let Perris ruin his name." She met Jake's eyes in the moonlight, so grateful for his caring and support. "Thank you for offering to help me."

He didn't say anything for several beats, then he nodded toward the B & B's front door. "You should go back inside. It's getting late, and I know you'll have another early day tomorrow."

Yes, she would. "Billy Hutchins is coming by around eight to deliver a load of campfire wood. I need to be there to pay him." She knew he wouldn't like what she said next. "Jake, I'm going to move back home tomorrow."

He sighed heavily. "You won't reconsider?"

"No. And please…no more escort service, okay? I made it all the way to Virginia and back without a problem or a police detail."

"Which made everyone who cares about you uneasy," he said. "If I could have gone with you, I would have."

Rachel fought the powerful urge to step into his

arms and thank him. But for some reason she couldn't fathom, something was off with him tonight, and she sensed the hug wouldn't be welcomed. That made her feel…empty. "I can get to the valley on my own. The man who burned my home is a coward. Everything that happened occurred at night, and it's only a five-mile drive. I'll be fine."

"Okay. Then I guess I'll say good night. Just be careful."

"I will." Then wishing the evening had ended on a warmer, more personal note, she went back inside and shut the door.

Jake slid behind the wheel of his truck, started the engine, then pulled on his headlights and stared through the windshield. He should drive away and not look back. He hadn't been looking for a relationship when he met her, but despite his best efforts, he seemed to have fallen into one. And there was no good reason for it. There were a lot of pretty women out there—even a few who enjoyed nature as much as he did. He wasn't a narcissist, but he knew he could find someone to spend time with if he wanted. He just hadn't "wanted" until recently.

But Rachel was out of reach, and it was futile to spend time hoping for something that wasn't going to happen. Besides, they were far from compatible on the religion issue. The man she'd married had been a devout Christian, while Jake's faith was iffy at best. He had a hard time believing in a merciful all-seeing, all-knowing deity who purportedly loved children when his sister had been violated, then left to die like a discarded rag doll in the street. No, he and Rachel weren't a good match. Even though the chemistry was there, she'd eventually want more from him in the faith department than he was able to give.

Dropping the truck into gear, he rolled to the bottom of the driveway, turned left and headed for home. He'd gone a quarter of a mile when the lights from the Tall Spruce Travel Lodge blinked a welcome. Lips thinning, he made the right turn into the lot and parked beside a shiny black Corvette.

A minute later, he'd crossed the asphalt and climbed the stairs to the outdoor entrance to room 214. She answered the door as soon as he knocked, which made him think she'd seen him pull into the lot.

"Hi," she said quietly, once again opening the door wide.

"Hi," he repeated. "You were right. We should talk."

TEN

Tired after another sleepless night, Rachel worked up a smile for young Billy Hutchins as she parked beside her camp store and got out. He stood in the bed of his old, red Chevy truck, tossing bundles of split firewood to the cause of her insomnia—a brown-eyed, broad-shouldered game protector who caught and stacked the wood against the far side of the store. When they were finished, she'd post her Burn Where You Buy signs, a plea from the forestry service aimed at campers who transported wood from other areas. Wood that could contain harmful emerald ash borers.

"Hey, Mrs. P.," Billy called with a smile

"Hey, Billy," Rachel called back. "Looks like you're nearly finished."

"Yep," he said, tossing another bundle to Jake. "Just a few more."

Billy was a good-looking kid in a concert T-shirt and fashionably ripped jeans, and wore his flowing blond mane in a style reminiscent of the '80s big-hair bands. Supplying local campgrounds with firewood put a few dollars in his pocket during the summer—money he'd eventually take to trade school to learn carpentry. He'd worked part-time at the lumber mill for a couple of months, but when the economy took a dive, eighteen-year-old Billy had been one of the first to be laid off.

Rachel walked to the truck, feeling a bittersweet twinge when Jake sent her a half smile. She missed his touch, missed his kisses. Missed sleeping the night through because she didn't know what was going on with him. She sent a wobbly smile back, then gave her attention to Billy. "Got an invoice for me, Billy?"

"Yeah. It's in my truck on the dashboard. It's not fancy, but it's something in writing."

"Great," she said, pulling open the door to retrieve it, then shutting it again. "Cash okay?"

"Works for me," he said, then grinned at Jake. "I offered to split with Jake, but he told me earlier that he'd rather have coffee."

Rachel smiled again. "I see. I think that can be arranged."

When Billy had been paid and moved on to his next customer, Rachel poured piping-hot coffee into a foam takeout cup, then carried it outside. Jake had just whistled for Maggie. "Here you go. Your cut of Billy's wages."

"Thanks. Actually, I enjoyed giving him a hand," Jake returned. "It gave me something to do until you showed up."

"Oh?" He had something to discuss with her?

"Yeah," he said frowning. "I got a call a few minutes ago from a guy who saw his neighbor's kids shoot a deer last night, so I have to run. It looks like the summer grilling season's begun. Anyway, when I get back, maybe we should put together a list of Donner's enemies and come up with a plan—if you want."

"I definitely want."

"Okay, then I'll see you later." He moved toward his vehicle, opened the door and set his coffee in a cup holder. "Hopefully, Perris will find someone else to annoy today."

"God willing," Rachel said quietly. But despite the fact that he was coming back, she still felt that uncomfortable distance between them again as he waved and drove off. And it hurt.

She was preparing to go back inside when Joe Reston drove up in the golf cart, his heavy cologne almost staining the morning air. "Billy left already?"

"Yes, just a few minutes ago. He had more deliveries to make. I understand you two worked together at the mill."

"Yeah, we did. He's a nice kid—good worker. Then the layoffs started." He blew out a breath. "But I guess it doesn't make sense to cut oak when the companies we supply aren't building furniture." Easing off the brake, he let the cart roll slowly. "But like the old-timers say, it's always darkest before the dawn."

Old-timers. That lightbulb in Rachel's mind came on. And suddenly she couldn't wait for Jake to get back.

"See you, Rachel."

"See you, Joe."

When Jake and Maggie came inside at three o'clock, she'd just finished arranging to have the campground's small pool readied for the season. She maintained the chemical levels, but the initial job was always left to professionals. Actually, it had been a day of phone calls. Earlier, she'd called Ben to thank him for the hardware for her door, and Beau Travis for hanging it.

"How did it go with the young outlaws?" she asked

as Maggie scooted behind the counter to have her ears scratched.

"No dice—couldn't make an arrest. But I called my new friend Billy and asked him to keep his ear to the ground. Hopefully, the next time local teens decide to go grocery shopping for venison, I'll know about it." Rachel extended a writing tablet, and Jake wandered over to the counter to take it. When he'd scanned the two names on the very short list, he looked at her. "I thought you said Donner had messed with a lot of people."

"He did. But trading insults, refusing to pay a bill or getting all rummed up and tearing through a farmer's hay field doesn't seem like grounds for murder. I listed the obvious ones. Jillian because of the beatings, and Will Trehern because he owned the land, and wouldn't sell it to me while he was still alive. Maybe Will got tired of seeing Jillian's bruises, did the deed, and buried Bryce where he wouldn't be found until Will was in the ground, too."

Jake dropped the tablet on the counter. "Did you tell Trehern that you planned to develop it?"

"Yes. So if he did kill Bryce—and knew the land would be excavated—maybe he wanted Jillian to know that he loved her enough to end her torment. Or maybe he just wanted her to have closure so she could get on with her life."

"Makes sense," he said, but then his rugged features lined. "I need to ask you something, but I don't want you to get upset."

She studied him for a moment. "Okay. What do you want to know?"

"Since you're convinced of Jillian's innocence and

listed her anyway, shouldn't David be included? Was there other trouble between him and Donner that you didn't mention? Something Perris could find out about and use to make a strong case?"

She didn't like the question, but it was a fair one if they were going to examine all of the possibilities. "No. If there'd been any other trouble, I would have known. David and I didn't keep secrets from each other." She nodded at the tablet. "The third and fourth spots on the page will go to the married woman Bryce was seeing, and her husband. I just don't know their names—yet."

"You said 'yet' as though you'll know who they are soon."

"I'm hopeful. Today when I was talking to Joe Reston, he used the phrase 'old-timers.' We need to talk to Elmer Fox."

Jake smiled a little. "The same Elmer Fox who can't wait to chew my head off over the deer management policy?"

"The same. He's a darling man, and he'd do anything for anyone. But if the information's out there, he'll have it. Elmer's the local clearing house for gossip and innuendo."

Jake shrugged. "Okay, then. Want to take a ride?"

"I certainly do." She glanced down at Maggie who seemed to be monitoring their conversation. "Come on, girl. The Frosty Freeze just opened. Maybe we can stop for ice cream on the way back."

Tall, bony Elmer Fox spent much of his time honoring the Lord, helping people and quizzing unsuspecting contestants on trivia—and the rest of it growling about the "gull-danged" things people did. Rachel knew he was going to be in a "gull-dang" mood when she spotted him walking up the dirt driveway to his hundred-and-thirty-year-old, dark green two-story. He carried a slim wooden pole with a spike sticking out of the bottom—and a bag nearly overflowing with litter.

A minute later, Jake had parked and the three of them were facing Elmer. He nodded at Jake, then took time to welcome Rachel and smile at the dog before he launched into a diatribe about litterbug kids who didn't have the courtesy God gave rice. Eventually, they were invited to sit on his front porch to look out on a sea of hand-painted signs. The backs were blank. The fronts were memorable. Most of them decried local government; others were more universal: Honor Our Vets. Trust in the Lord and Be Saved. No Trespassing. A decades-old sign draped with faded red, white and blue bunting simply said: ROSS PEROT.

"Always been partial to dogs," Elmer said, affectionately ruffling Maggie's fur. He'd taken a seat on the worn wooden rocker, leaving the porch swing for Jake and Rachel. "Had two beagles once. They were fine dogs. Never chased cars, never chased deer." The pale blue eyes behind his rimless eyeglasses sent Jake an extended look. "You here to talk about the deer, Mr. Game Warden?"

"No, sir, I'm not. But we'll do that sometime soon."

Rachel eased forward. It was time to get down to business. "Elmer, Jake and I are hoping you can help us with some information. I imagine you've heard about the body that was uncovered at my place."

"Max Donner's boy, Bryce," Elmer said in an aging rasp. "Even babies in their cribs are yammering about that. It was a bad end to a life."

"Yes, it was, and someone needs to pay for it. But Jake and I think the police should be looking at more than one person who had a motive."

Elmer's gaze sharpened. "More than one person? Who are they tryin' to hang this on?"

Rachel sighed. "A good man who couldn't have done it. Chief Perris said he's not ruling out anyone else, but..."

When she told him about Perris's visit and her need to clear David's name, Elmer got his blood up again. "That's what happens when a town hands a badge over to a big-city stranger. That young pup doesn't know a thing about the people he's here to protect." He jerked an annoyed look at Jake. "You gonna help her out with this? Take care of her? Because she's gonna take some guff over it. Folks don't like other folks nosin' around in their business."

"I'm in it for as long as it takes," Jake assured him.

Elmer slapped the arm of his rocker. "All right, then. What can I tell you?"

"We need the names of anyone who might have wanted Bryce Donner dead."

The old man laughed until he wheezed. "You don't want a list, boy. You want the county phone book. There weren't too many folks who liked him. He cut wages at the mill, got himself in trouble with the union, drank too much and spent time with too many women who didn't belong to him."

"Do you remember anything radical happening with the mill employees or the union?"

"Depends on what you mean by radical. Tar paper nails showed up in young Donner's tires, and there were a lot of busted windows at the mill. I believe he had to change his phone number, too, when crank calls got to be a problem. But that goes on during strikes."

"Nothing worse?"

"Nothin' to justify puttin' a bullet in a man's head."

Rachel grimaced. "What about the women, Elmer? Do you know who they were and if any of them were married?" When Elmer hesitated she went on. "We'll be discreet. We won't share the information with anyone but Perris. Elmer, he needs to know that David wasn't the only one who had trouble with Bryce."

Elmer rubbed a liver-spotted hand over a day's growth of white whiskers and rocked for a few moments. "I recall there bein' some single ladies. Louise Sauder was sweet on him for a while, and Allie Kubyak liked him some. But I can think of only one of 'em who was married. Saw her misbehavin' myself." He raised a cautioning finger. "But I ain't accusing her or her man of anything."

Rachel shot Jake a brief, excited look. "We understand that. Go on, Elmer."

"I was pickin' huckleberries down near the Restons' camp when I cut through the backyard and saw him and her smoochin' it up out there by the water pump."

"Him and her?" Rachel asked.

"Tammy and Donner. I heard it said they were friendly for a long time, too."

"Did Joe know?"

"Can't say," Elmer replied. "But if he did, there woulda been trouble over it. Bryce Donner and Joe Reston were friends."

Rachel released a long breath when they were back in the truck and on their way. Wind through Jake's open window filled the cab with fresh air and drowned out the barely audible music from a country station. "Well, that was enlightening."

"To say the least. Now you have another name to add to your list. Maybe two if the relationship went sour, and Tammy wasn't happy about it." He glanced at her. "You've probably noticed the gun rack in the back of her truck."

"And the bumper stickers," Rachel replied.

"Well, none of it's window dressing," Jake said, steering around a pothole in the road. "I ran into her last month at the Sportsmen's Club's firing range. She's a crack shot with a rifle, and nearly as good with a pistol."

"Lovely. Now my mind is positively swimming with crime-of-passion scenarios." Maggie poked her red head over the back of the seat, and Rachel stroked her silky neck. "Do you think I should contact my guests again?"

"And say what?"

She raised an imaginary phone to her ear and spoke wryly. "Hello, Mrs. Smith. This is Rachel Patterson. I called last week to tell you that my home had burned to the ground? Well, now it seems that the fire was arson and someone has me in their crosshairs. Also—and there's really no need for alarm—recently, a body was found on my land, and the killer could be one of the men I hired for campground security."

She dropped her hand to her lap.

Jake glanced across at her again. "What did Mrs. Smith say?"

"Nothing. She hung up as soon as I got to the arson."

Rachel turned to face him, straining her seat belt. "So what do I do now? Do I ask Joe to leave?"

"That's up to you. Just keep two things in mind." He didn't wait for her to ask what they were. "Reston might not have known about the affair. And Elmer was right about the people in this town—or in any town, for that matter. There's going to be trouble if your friends and neighbors find out we're poking into their pasts."

"Don't I know it," she replied glumly.

They'd reached a straight stretch on the wooded road, and a quarter of a mile ahead, a horse-drawn Amish buggy turned right onto a side road leading to the sect's farming settlement. Rachel spoke quickly. "Jake, take the next right."

A trace of crime-fighter amusement tinged his voice. "You mean, 'Follow that buggy'?"

"Yes. I've been meaning to ask Nora Zook if she wants to sell her fudge and candy at the camp store this season, and haven't gotten around to seeing her yet."

"And the Amish don't have phones."

"Right. Phones are 'proud.' I won't be long."

The Zook farm was like the others in the settlement—lush and green and neatly tended, with colorful quilts on the clotheslines, a barn and silo scraping the sky, and several outbuildings and birdhouses for good measure. The smell of freshly cut lumber rode the air, and a sign at the bottom of the dirt driveway said "Amish-Made Sheds."

The young driver they'd followed to the Zook property leaped down from his black buggy and walked to Jake's truck. In his early teens, Jonathan "Yonnie" Zook was dressed in plain black pants with suspenders and a blue shirt. His chin was bare, and thick brown curls stuck out from under his straw hat. He smiled when Rachel and Jake got out, leaving Maggie to watch from the open window.

"Hi, Yonnie," Rachel said. When they'd shaken hands, she introduced him to Jake.

Jake offered his hand, too. "*Guten Tag,* Yonnie."

Yonnie raised his eyebrows, then repeated the greeting. His English was heavily accented, owing to a traditional upbringing by his parents and a community that spoke nothing but German when among themselves. "You know the plain talk," he said.

"Only a few words," Jake replied. When I was in college, I did a paper—an article—on Amish living. There were Amish families nearby, and eventually I was invited to stay with one of them for ten days."

Yonnie remained amused. "You did the milking?"

"I did a bit of everything. Shoveled manure, helped fill a silo, fed corn into a cutter. Attended a church service."

Yonnie nodded knowingly, a smile at the corners of his lips. "I think three hours of prayer was long for you."

Jake chuckled. "Yeah, it was long. But the music—the hymns—were nice."

"You made us look good in your paper?"

"Yes, I did."

Yonnie nodded again. "*Gut.* I'll call my *mutter* for Rachel." He sent Jake the sly, calculated look of a salesman. "While they talk, you must look at the fine sheds we build. You'll want one for yourself."

Dusk was approaching when they finally left the Zooks' farm with a snitz pie for Rachel and a warm *"guten nacht"* for Jake, who'd ordered one of Yonnie's sheds and a playhouse for Greg and Julie's baby to grow into.

"You're full of surprises," Rachel said.

"How so?"

"You were almost-Amish for ten days. You never mentioned it."

He turned on his headlights. "That's because the secret to being boring is to tell everything."

As if he could ever be boring. "So what did you really think?"

"I won't lie to you. It was a lot of work, and getting up at four-thirty in the morning for breakfast was a major culture shock. But looking back, I really did enjoy my time with them."

"Thinking about converting?"

He smiled. "I think ten days with me was about all they could handle. But I wouldn't mind feeling that contented—that peaceful. I think the simpler our lives are, the easier it is to concentrate on the important things."

Night had fallen in earnest by the time Jake left for home, and the moon that had been so bright the night before was blanketed in clouds. From somewhere, the cry of a screech owl pierced the stillness.

Feeling a sudden chill, Rachel closed the window over the screen in her bedroom, then called Maggie from the store area. But as the dog bounded inside, then leaped onto her sleeping bag and air mattress, she knocked over a box of clothing Rachel hadn't yet found a place for.

A gift-wrapped package fell out.

For a second, Rachel froze. Then she shook her head and called herself an idiot. Killers didn't send gifts.

Scooting Maggie out of the way, she lowered herself to the mattress and picked up the package that was obviously a book. There was a note attached, and she smiled as she scanned it:

> *We smuggled this in with your things as you were packing this morning. Be safe, and if you get tired of sleeping on the floor, there's a bed for you here at the Blackberry.*
>
> *Love, Jenna and Aunt Molly*

Rachel unwrapped the Bible, then opened it to a page Jenna had bookmarked. There was a dot of yellow highlighter beside a scripture verse.

> *Fear not, for I am with you. Be not dismayed,*
> *for I am your God.*
> *I will strengthen you, I will help you. I will*
> *uphold you in my righteous right hand.*
>
> —Isaiah 41:18

Rachel stroked the page. "Thank you, God, for my good friends and family," she whispered. "Please bless them all—and tonight, Jake especially. You probably heard him say he wouldn't mind feeling the kind of peace and contentment he saw in the Amish community. So even though he's confident and secure in his life, he knows something's missing. That something is a relationship with You." She paused, becoming thoughtful. "I don't believe he's completely opposed to the idea—just hesitant to reach out. Please give him the nudge he needs to find his way back to You."

* * *

The next morning, she was slipping into one of the two dresses she'd purchased when she moved to the Blackberry when she heard the high-pitched beep that signaled a visitor. Or more precisely, a vehicle because the sensor detected only metal. Quickly buckling the belt on her knitted, hunter-green shirt dress, she followed a barking Maggie to the front door and peered through the window beside it. A moment later, Jake's dark blue Ram truck rolled down the hill and eased into a parking space.

She kept her emotions in check as he got out, took a bag of dog food from the truck's bed, then walked toward the store. The brown dress pants he wore with a cream-colored shirt and brown dress boots wasn't too big a departure from his usual outdoorsy look. She unlocked the doors and backed up as he came inside.

"You look nice," she said.

"Thanks," he said, smiling. "You look better." He put Maggie's food on the floor and scanned her outfit. Everything from her hoop earrings to the gold buckle at her waist and the three unfastened buttons at her hem that made walking easier. "Nice dress."

She couldn't stop a smile of her own. "Thank you." She was about to ask why he was all dressed up when he added, "But your throat looks a little bare." Jake walked over to her. "Turn around."

"Why?"

"Just turn around. Please."

"Okay." She showed him her back. "Do I have to count to ten or anything?"

"Nope. Just hold still."

She heard a slight rustling, then he reached in front

of her, and she caught a glimpse of gold. She knew what it was before he finished fastening the chain around her neck. Emotional tears stung her eyes, and Rachel raised a hand to her throat to touch the narrow filigreed cross, feel its golden weight. "Oh, Jake."

Turning her around, he smiled down into her eyes. "You're welcome. Now don't wreck the moment by offering me a check."

He didn't take his warm hands from her shoulders. He didn't step away. And suddenly the room seemed to shrink around them, and Rachel's heartbeat quickened. Kiss me, she whispered in her mind as she watched thoughts cloud his eyes. Kiss me and tell me that you care. Give me a reason to step into your arms and tell you how deeply you touch me with your kindness and everything else you are. Tell me you're not going back to Heather. Tell me.

But with a look of regret that mirrored Rachel's own deep disappointment, he stepped back and mustered a smile meant to break the mood. "If we leave soon, we can probably stop for coffee and Danish at the diner before church."

Hope rose in the midst of her regret. "You're going to church?"

"No, I'm taking *you* to church," he said clarifying. "If I happen to stay for the service instead of waiting outside, I wanted to be dressed appropriately." He looked at Maggie. "You stay here and hold the fort."

Was he being completely truthful? Rachel wondered. Or was driving her to church a stepping stone back to God? Either way, he'd be sitting beside her in the pew. It was up to Reverend Landers to take it from there.

* * *

The church bells pealed out a goodbye as Rachel and Jake filed out, shook hands with Reverend and Mrs. Landers, then walked toward the parking lot. They hadn't gotten far when someone called to Jake and he excused himself for a moment. Rachel took the opportunity to talk with Jillian Donner, who was also moving toward the lot. They'd prayed for Bryce during the service today, and Reverend Landers had offered the congregation's sympathies. But Rachel had yet to offer her personal condolences.

Jillian was a tiny woman, smart and pretty, with skin the color of flour and a soft, agreeable manner. Despite her wealth and the fact that she was only two years older than Rachel, she wore her blond hair in a bun, and chose colors and clothing that didn't call attention to herself. Today she was dressed in beige.

Rachel spoke quietly as she approached her. "Hi, Jillian. I'm so sorry about Bryce."

"Thanks," she replied, acceptance rather than remorse in her voice. "He wasn't a saint, but he didn't deserve what happened to him."

"No, he didn't. Hopefully there'll be an arrest soon."

"From your lips to God's ears." She brushed a wisp of blond hair away from her face. "Chief Perris stopped by to see me the other day. He wanted to know when I'd last seen Bryce, and if I still had the note he'd left." She shrugged. "I assume you've heard about the note. Everyone else in town has."

Rachel nodded. There was no point in denying it. "You still had it?"

"No, I'd thrown it away long ago. I guess he wanted it

for handwriting comparison." Her brows came together. "Funny, I don't remember thinking that it *wasn't* his handwriting—well, printing—but then, Bryce wasn't the kind to leave me notes. Romantic or otherwise. But if he didn't write it, that means that someone else left it with his ring on my kitchen table. I don't like thinking that his killer was in my home while I slept."

Rachel knew exactly how she felt. Someone had visited her home, too, while she was unaware. "Reverend Landers said there'd be a memorial service in a few days. I'll try to make it."

"Thanks." When she nodded toward the church, Rachel looked that way, too. Jake was talking with Ben Caruthers now. "Nate's inside talking to the reverend about the service right now. We'd like to have a dinner afterward in the community room, but I doubt many people would come." She smiled then. "You probably know that Nate and I have been seeing each other for a while. Now that I know I'm free, we can start making plans."

"Wedding plans?"

Jillian nodded. "Not immediately. That wouldn't feel right. But maybe in the fall."

"How wonderful," Rachel murmured. If anyone deserved a good life with a good man after living with Bryce, she did. But that thought brought his murder to mind again. "Jillian," she said hesitantly. "I hope you'll forgive me for backtracking for a moment, but... did Perris ask you who might have had a reason to kill Bryce?"

"Yes, and I gave him a few names, but he was interested in only two of them. Me and my uncle Will." She smiled wryly when Rachel looked startled. "Yes, I included myself. But I didn't do it, so that leaves Will—who hated Bryce for reasons I don't think I have to mention."

No, she didn't.

Jillian sighed. "Perris thinks Bryce was killed somewhere else because they couldn't find a bullet."

Which meant someone had to have physically moved and buried him. At ninety pounds, Jillian couldn't have managed it. Still, one good thing had come out of their conversation. Perris was looking at other suspects.

They'd said their goodbyes and Rachel was moving away when Jillian stopped her. "Rachel?"

"Yes?"

Jillian walked to her. "I probably shouldn't tell you this, but there was another name Perris mentioned. Not a name I gave him. One of his own." Her face softened apologetically. "Rachel, he asked a lot of questions about David."

"What's wrong?" Jake asked minutes later as she crossed the pavement to him.

Rachel couldn't keep the anger out of her voice. "Perris is at it again, and I'm so upset I could chew nails. If he can't prove that Will Trehern killed Bryce, I think he'll pin this on David to save himself the trouble of a real investigation."

"You already knew that was a possibility."

"But now he's sharing his ridiculous theories with other people." Tears filled her eyes. "He doesn't deserve this, Jake! The only problem he ever had with Bryce was over me."

Jake opened the passenger's door and nodded for her to get in. "Come on. I'll take you back home."

It was a silent ride. They were nearly to the campground when Rachel looked over at Jake's serious expression and realized that her outburst had really put a damper on the day. She forced herself to concentrate on other things.

"I saw you talking with Ben. What did he want?"

"There's a warranty on your door locks. He said he'd mail it. I was going to pick it up after I left the elementary school tomorrow, but he said he might not be around. I guess he's taking some time off."

"What's going on at the elementary school?"

"An assembly. The deputy who called me over asked if I could sub for him. His wife's having some problems with her pregnancy, and he wants to be with her while her doctor runs some tests. It's their first."

Rachel softened her voice. "That has to be scary for them. I'll add them to my prayer list. I've always regretted that—" She stopped abruptly.

"What?"

"Nothing," she said, then forced a smile. It was time to leave the past behind or she'd never have a future. "It's nothing."

Jake walked around the store, picking up odds and ends from the shelves, then putting them back while he waited for Rachel to change her clothes. He'd managed to keep his lousy mood hidden for the past few hours, but it hadn't been easy. She was on a quest, and she wouldn't be happy until David was cleared. But he was tired of hearing the man's name, and in all honesty, part of him was beginning to wonder if Saint David actually *had* murdered Bryce Donner. It wouldn't be the first time a quiet man had kept a secret hidden. TV and the newspapers were full of stories about mild-mannered loners.

Suddenly, his thoughts took a one-eighty. David couldn't have done it. If he had, that meant the prowler episode and the fire at Rachel's home had nothing to do with Bryce Donner's death—and everyone believed the events were connected. Dead men didn't rise from the grave to cover their crimes. He said as much to Rachel when she stepped back into the room wearing a purple T-shirt tucked into faded jeans.

Her green eyes lit excitedly. "That's right. And Perris believes all three events are connected, too." She strode toward the phone behind the lunch counter. "I'm calling him."

"Let me say goodbye first. I need to look over my workshop on reptiles and get some brochures together for the assembly tomorrow."

She stopped, and her smiled faltered. "Oh. Okay." She walked him to the door. "It seems as though all I ever do is thank you."

And it seemed as though all he ever did was leave. He opened the screen door.

"Jake?" She touched his arm, searched his eyes. But he kept his hands to himself. He wouldn't back away completely because she could still be in danger. But there would be no more touching. He didn't need another kick in the heart. "I'll talk to you soon, Rachel."

She moved her hand. "You, too," she said quietly.

He'd stopped to give Maggie some attention when something she'd said earlier came to mind again. Glutton for punishment that he was, he lifted his voice. She was standing in the open screen door. "Can I ask you something?"

"You can ask me anything," she replied.

"You started to say something today after church, but didn't finish. You wanted kids."

He watched her step outside, fold her arms across her chest, then leave the stoop and walk over to join him. The cross he'd given her lay golden and gleaming against her purple T-shirt; David's gold wedding band gleamed beside it every time she reached up to touch the cross.

"Yes, I would have liked that. But it didn't happen. How about you? Ever think about having a few little Campbells?"

"Isn't that what most men want? A family?" But without a wife to bear them, there was zero chance of his being a father anytime soon.

"Did Heather want them?"

He didn't answer right away because some ridiculous part of him was suddenly feeling a flicker of hope. "I don't know. Whenever I raised the subject, we ended up talking about cruises—and anything else that had nothing to do with diapers and middle-of-the-night feedings. I don't think she was interested then."

She spoke tentatively. "And now?"

Was that disappointment in her voice? He had to know, and he couldn't tell. "We talked before she went home. Things aren't working out with Mark."

"Then she's gone?"

"For the moment. She said she likes the area." He considered what he was about to say next, then said it and waited for her reaction. "She wants to try again."

Her reply wasn't the one he was looking for, even though it took her a few moments to respond. "People change," she said quietly. "Maybe…maybe you should give her another chance."

No way on God's green earth. But finally seeing the writing on the wall, he snatched back a little of his pride and said grimly, "Maybe I should."

ELEVEN

Rachel awoke Monday morning to a whine and a cold wet nose against her cheek. She smiled tiredly into Maggie's brown eyes. "Good morning to you, too," she said. "Need to go out?" Maggie padded to the game room's door and waited.

"Okay," Rachel said, rising. "Let's go." Slipping on the blue robe Jenna had donated, she went into the store and opened both doors. Maggie bounded out into the thin drizzle. It was a dreary day. Storm clouds had moved in overnight, blocking out the sun. Rachel sighed. She needed sunshine today because the longer she stood looking out at the rain, the more she thought about last night's conversation with Jake.

Was he really going to give Heather another chance? Or was he thinking about settling for less to have the children he wanted? At thirty-six did he think he was running out of time? That kind of betrayal would be difficult to forgive. She doubted that she could.

Maggie loped out of the woods across from the store, then ran back inside, shaking the rain from her coat as the alarm near the top of the driveway sounded. A moment later, Joe Reston rolled past the screen door to start his seven-to-three shift. Rachel returned his wave, then closed the inside door and went to the galley to feed Maggie. There was no point in starting the coffee-maker. Jake would be at the elementary school today. He wouldn't be stopping in until later. If at all.

She'd finished stocking her shelves and was making copies of the campground rules and regulations a few hours later when the phone rang. Tammy Reston was trying to reach her husband, and she sounded anxious.

"I hope I didn't get you at a bad time, Rachel, but I can't get him on his cell phone."

"Yes, I know. There *is* no cell service once you get to the bottom of Crocker Hill." She carried the handset to the door and let Maggie out again. It was still cloudy, but the rain had stopped. "Joe's making his rounds now, but I can track him down, or leave a note at the cabin the security guys are using. He'll head back there eventually."

"That's okay. I don't want to put you out."

Maybe not, but she'd called the store hoping to reach him, and she still sounded tense. "It's no trouble at all. I planned to post flyers at the cabins today anyway. I'll just leave him a note asking him to call you from the store."

"If you're sure…"

"I am. Oh, one more thing as long as we're talking. Can you add two more pies to my weekly order? A cherry and an apple?"

"I'd be glad to," she returned. "Thanks, Rachel."

"You're welcome. Take care."

Soon, armed with thumb tacks, laminated copies and a note for Joe, Rachel hiked through the wet grass to her five A-frame log cabins. Situated in a field behind the playground, they were tenderfoot favorites because of their amenities and the privacy they afforded. They were also equipped with small, rustic porches and outdoor charcoal grills. Within minutes, she'd tacked copies of the rules to the back of the wooden doors on cabins one and two, and crossed the yard to the third. Joe Reston's truck was parked in the short driveway beside the nearly ground-level porch.

"Joe?" she called, stepping onto the porch. "Are you in there?" She smelled coffee through the screen door—saw a mug and box of donuts sitting on the pine picnic table inside. But the golf cart was nowhere to be seen, so she knocked once for good measure and went in.

Some campgrounds in the area rented cabins with sleeping quarters only. Hers offered indoor plumbing, small showers and microwaves as well as rough-hewn pine beds with foam mattresses. All the comforts of home if home wasn't too fancy.

Moving quickly, she dropped Joe's note beside his coffee mug, tacked a laminated list of rules to the back of the inside door and left. She wasn't sure why she turned to look at his rain-splashed truck. Maybe because he'd backed it in so close to the cabin, the side mirror barely missed the railing. But she looked.

What she saw on the front seat made her go still.

Quickly, she left the porch and strode to the driver's side window for a second look. Chills ran the length of her. Tossed across the seat was a navy blue hooded windbreaker with an emblem on the back, half of which was hidden. Looking around nervously, she opened the door, straightened the jacket…and saw her "rabbit's head." Two white bowling pins flying away from a light blue ball!

Rachel ran pell-mell across the long field to the camp

store, her wet sneakers kicking through dandelions, her lungs on fire. Reaching it, she burst inside and rushed behind the lunch counter for the cordless handset and phone book. Her hands shook. She couldn't call 9-1-1. There was no proof that Reston had done anything wrong. She had to speak to Perris—regardless of the fact that he'd been his usual derisive self yesterday when she'd phoned to offer near-proof of David's innocence.

She sank to a stool and dialed. A moment later, secretary and daytime dispatcher Sarah French answered the phone in a pleasant singsong. "Charity Police Department. This is Sarah. How may I direct your call?"

"Sarah, it's Rachel Patterson. I need to speak to Chief Perris immediately. Is he there?"

Picking up on her tension, Sarah responded quickly. "He just went to the diner for takeout. Is there another problem at the campground, Rachel? Fish is here. He can be down there in a—"

"Thanks, but I really need to speak to Perris. Can you have him call me when he gets back? And please stress how important it is that I speak to him. I'm not one of his favorite people. There's a chance he could 'forget' to make the call."

Sarah lowered her voice. "I'll put the call through myself, Rachel. He shouldn't be any longer than ten minutes or so. What's your number there so I don't have to look it up?"

Rachel gave her the number, then thanked her again and sat back to wait. It was only a few minutes, but it seemed like forever until the phone rang and Perris's cool baritone came on the line. "What can I do for you today, Mrs. Patterson?"

Rachel took a stabilizing breath. First things first.

Then she'd connect the dots. "You need to look into Joe Reston's whereabouts the night Tim Decker's bulldozer was vandalized."

"And why do I need to do that?"

"Because I believe Joe stayed down here that night. He has a camp a few miles down the road." She drew a shaky breath. "If he's my prowler, and my prowler is the arsonist...there's a chance he also killed Bryce Donner." She backed up. "I saw a hooded jacket in Joe's truck a few minutes ago. The emblem on the back was a bowling ball between two pins. I believe that's what I saw that night. And Joe Reston had a motive."

Perris released a long-suffering sigh. "Okay, what's the motive? What would make Reston kill a friend?"

He knew Joe Reston and Bryce had been friends? Had he already questioned someone about Joe? "A woman," she replied. "Tammy Reston was having an affair with Bryce before he died. Joe wouldn't have liked that."

"*If* he'd known about it," Perris said.

"All I'm asking you to do is follow up," she said more sharply than she'd intended. She was tired of butting her head against Perris's brick wall. "Isn't that your job?"

It was the wrong thing to say to a man who'd already lost patience with her. "Let me save you some time, Nancy Drew," he said, ice in his voice. "Someone came forward two days ago with this information. I've already spoken to Mr. Reston and he has a rock-solid alibi for the night of the vandalism. That alibi has agreed to testify on his behalf if it becomes necessary. I assured this person that it wasn't."

A woman. Tammy was right. Joe had been with a woman that night. Sighing, Rachel propped her elbow on the counter and massaged the tension over her eyes. But...who would have been privy to that information? And who'd told Perris about Bryce and Tammy's affair? Elmer?

The hairs on her arms prickled. The only person she could think of who might have steered Perris toward Joe Reston was Tammy. Flash-fire thoughts raced through her mind. Could Tammy have been in love with Bryce? And upon learning of Bryce's murder, had she gone to Perris, heartsick and angry, and spilled everything? Especially if she believed—or knew—that Joe was cheating again? *Yes.*

"Now if you don't mind, Mrs. Patterson," Perris concluded, "I'd like to eat my lunch before it gets any colder."

Wincing, Rachel yanked herself out of her thoughts. "Of course. Thank you for your time."

"You're welcome. I trust we won't be speaking about this again."

Rachel pressed the disconnect button on the handset, exhaled raggedly, then spun slowly on her stool. She felt horrible. Worse than horrible. And she could cross Perris off her list as an ally the next time she needed one—not that he'd ever been one. At least she knew the head of her security team wasn't a kill—

Big Joe Reston tore open the screen door, nearly ripping it from its hinges, then stormed across the room. A sick feeling pooled in Rachel's stomach. Dear God, how long had he been there! How much had he heard? She tried to rise from the stool, but he was on her in a moment, slamming his meaty hands on the bar on either side of her and pinning her to the counter.

He jammed his beet-red face close to hers. "Where

do you get off sticking your nose in other people's lives?"

"Joe, I'm sorry! Let me—"

"Explain?" he thundered. "It's a little late for explanations when you accuse a man of murder. Do you know how many people have jackets like mine? Dozens! And for your information, I didn't kill Donner. But if I'd known about him and Tammy, he would've wished he was dead." Swearing, he levered himself away, bounced her wadded note off her lap and stalked to the door. "Now if you'll excuse me, I need to talk to my wife. You can mail my paycheck."

Shaken to her core, Rachel waited until the door slammed behind him and the golf cart took off. Then she grabbed the handset from the counter, found Tammy's cell phone number in her caller history and hit Redial. She had to reach Tammy before Joe did! A recorded voice told her to leave a message. She flipped through the phone book again—dialed the sporting goods store. One ring…two rings…three.

"Pick up, Tammy," she said nervously. "Pick up."

A second answering machine kicked in. This time, Tammy's lilting honky-tonk thanked her for calling Reston's Sporting Goods and listed their hours. "We close for lunch at noon, but we'll be back at one. See you then!"

Rachel froze again as Joe Reston's truck roared up the driveway and fishtailed past the door. Seconds later that high-pitched beep sounded. He was flying!

Praying, begging God to keep Tammy safe, she tried the Reston home, then the diner and the Quick Mart… but to no avail. "Sweet Jesus, help her," she whispered fervently. "Please don't let Joe hurt her."

* * *

Jake carried a box of leftover brochures and his rattlesnake and copperhead models into his office, then shed his uniform and pulled on jeans and a white knit henley shirt. He shoved back the long sleeves—left the button placket open. After the assembly, he'd stayed behind to field questions and grab a late bite with the teachers in the cafeteria, but he thought the workshop had gone well. Hopefully when the kids headed to the local woods and parks in a few days, they'd be armed with enough information on poisonous snakes and other dangers to make theirs a safe, enjoyable summer.

Too bothered by the quiet, he returned to his office and checked his messages. There was a thank you from the school's principal and a reminder of an upcoming meeting from regional, but that was it. Not even an update from his mom on Julie's condition. He stood there for a moment, then frowning, strode to his screened-in back porch, filled a bucket with sunflower seeds and topped off his bird feeders.

His restlessness remained. He missed the sound of voices. That hadn't been the case for a long time. He'd preferred the quiet while he was purging Heather from his system and trying to find some balance in his life. But now...now the silence was just one more reminder that he was alone. Scowling, he took the empty bucket and scoop back to the porch. Then against every recent promise he'd made to himself, he took that mile-long walk to the campground. A romance was out, but they could still be friends.

Moth to a flame, a tiny voice chanted. Moth to a flame.

"Not this time," Jake murmured.

* * *

Jake's senses went on full alert as he approached the camp store and heard high-pitched shouting coming from inside. Then Tammy Reston burst through the screen door and headed for her idling black truck, her tears failing to douse the fire in her eyes. Rachel rushed out behind her, and Jake moved from a walk to a jog. What was going on?

"Tammy, wait!" Rachel cried. "Did he hurt you? Are you okay?"

Tammy whirled on her. "Are you blind? No, I'm not okay. Now leave me alone!" Her voice rose. "And find someone else to bake your pies!"

Jake tried to stop her. It was a mistake for her to drive when she was this upset. "Tammy, wait."

"No! Get out of my way or I'll have you charged with unlawful detention!" Straining the seams of her camouflage skirt, she swung into her ride and revved the engine, then spoke through the open window. "Watch your step, Jake. She'll chew you up and spit you out, too." Then she punched the gas and roared up the winding drive to the state route.

Jake turned to look at Rachel. She was leaning in defeat against the screen door, tears streaming down her cheeks. Beside her, Maggie whined softly and nudged Rachel's limp hand.

He crossed the driveway to her. Difficult as it was, he resisted the urge to take her in his arms. That had to be over. "Want to talk about it?" he asked quietly.

She shook her head no. "You'll hate me. I did something horrible. Something that can't be fixed."

"Come on," he said, easing her away from the door. "I'm not going to hate you, and it can't be that bad."

He ushered her inside, waited until she'd settled at the counter, then filled a glass with water from the tap and set it beside her. "What happened?"

Rachel took a napkin from the dispenser on the counter, blew her nose, then stuffed it in her jeans pocket. "Joe Reston didn't do it."

"Which? The prowling, the vandalism or Donner?"

"He didn't do any of them. Tammy wasn't involved, either." Drawing a trembling breath, she sobbed out the whole story. When she was through, she looked thoroughly beaten. "I'm so worried about Tammy."

And Jake was worried about *her*. She was one security man short now, and because the Atkins brothers were Joe's friends, there was a chance she'd lose them, too. "Okay," he said, "this is going to sound insensitive, but for my money, neither of the Restons should be pointing their fingers at the other. They both cheated. It's hard for me to dredge up any sympathy for them. When you make a promise, you keep it."

She looked at him with tired eyes. "Does that apply to you and Heather, too? You're ready to give her a second chance. At least that's what it sounded like last night."

He shook his head. Lies—implied or otherwise—never got anyone anywhere. What he'd said last night, he'd said to soothe his pride. If he looked like a sap admitting the truth, then so be it. "Heather and I are over. No second chances. She thinks I'll eventually change my mind, but she's wrong."

"It's hard to stop loving someone, Jake."

It certainly seemed that way for Rachel. "Only if it's been a good relationship. For me, love and trust go hand in hand; one can't exist without the other." He walked around to the front of the counter and lowered himself to the round blue stool next to her. He met her red-rimmed eyes. "You need to replace Joe."

She expelled a ragged breath. "Maybe not. In a matter of days, the kids I hired will be here. I'll just ask the Atkins brothers to cover from three to midnight and midnight to eight."

"Provided they don't quit out of loyalty to Joe."

Rachel nodded. "Yes."

"Do you want to bag this investigation of ours before we tick off someone else?"

"No. When I phoned him yesterday, Perris gave me a song and a dance about the possibility of a second person being in collusion with the killer. That means he's still not letting David—or me—off the hook." She swallowed. "I think he was just putting me in my place because he considered my concern interference. But I don't know for sure."

"Okay." He could do this. He could do it and still maintain some distance. Not the easiest of tasks because days ago, he'd issued an invitation and he was a man of his word. "One more thing. Before we dig in again and I forget, dinner will be later on Wednesday. I have another meeting. Would seven or seven-thirty work for you?"

"Dinner?"

"Lasagna. For your birthday."

Maybe she sensed that things had changed between them, or maybe she felt so low that she didn't think she deserved to be treated well, no matter who was doing the treating. Either way, she shook her head. "You don't have to do that." She touched her gold cross. "You've already given me a gift."

"I keep my promises, Rachel."

She searched his eyes—took a moment. "Okay. Okay, thank you. Just let Maggie and me know when dinner's almost ready. It doesn't matter what time. The campground's ready for guests, so there's not much left for me to do. I'm a free agent."

No, she wasn't, Jake thought, glad that truth had finally sunken in. And he couldn't fall in love with a woman who'd never be his completely. He just wished he wasn't already halfway there.

Needles of fear prickled his mind and belly as he rushed nervously from the diner clutching a foam cup of coffee. Rachel and her meddling game warden were looking into Donner's death, too—asking around about things that had happened five years ago. He'd overheard Elmer discussing it with his old cronies in the next booth, preening because he was helping them. Those needles swept through him, covering him like stings from ground bees. He needed to run! But, oh, how he needed to stay.

Sucking in a breath, he climbed into his SUV and set his coffee in a cup holder. Maybe Perris would get lazy and pin it on one of the dead men—make life easier for himself. If not David Patterson, then old Will Trehern. The way Donner had beaten Will's niece would have given the man just cause.

Maybe...maybe he could plant a few seeds—tell Perris that he'd seen Jillian Donner's bruises a number of times. Coming from a respected local merchant, that information could carry some weight.

Quickly easing into the light traffic, he drove to the Quick Mart, turned around and headed back toward the police station. He was about to pull into the stone-and-timber building's parking lot when he remembered something and he took off again. He couldn't do it. The TV crime shows he watched never failed to mention that criminals liked to insert themselves into investigations. He swallowed. Maybe he did have to leave.

TWELVE

Tuesday moved along without incident. No one threatened her or withdrew their friendship, no one quit and no one dumped a dead body on her property. Maggie padded along behind Rachel as she walked the floor, her phone to her ear. The sheer exuberance in Billy Hutchins's voice made Rachel smile. She had two graduating seniors and two returning college kids starting work Thursday, but she'd been so taken with Billy's courtesy, respect and willingness to work that she'd decided to offer him a job, too.

"It's not a lot of money," she continued, "but you can have all the pop and hot dogs you can handle, and you'll still have a few days free for cutting and delivering wood, if you want."

"Works for me, Mrs. P.," he answered happily. "Oh, man. This is a real gift. Thanks a lot!"

"You're welcome. Just be here tomorrow around four so you can meet the rest of the gang and get your schedule. I won't keep you long. We pull out the mowers and lawn tractor Thursday."

"I'll be there. Thanks again. Oh, and happy birthday tomorrow, in case I forget."

Rachel stared curiously at the handset before she

answered. "Thank you. How did you know it was my birthday?"

"Mr. Campbell told me when we were unloading wood Saturday. He said he's making dinner for you. Hope he can cook."

Rachel's heart did a silly flip-flop. Jake had said that? To Billy? Maybe she'd read him wrong last night. Maybe... She let herself hope just a little. "I'm not afraid. I'm guessing he knows his way around a kitchen. See you tomorrow, Billy."

"Yep, see you then."

Rachel hit the disconnect button, then strode behind the lunch counter to her little galley. She was about to return the receiver to the cradle when it rang in her hand. She checked the caller ID window and drew a breath. "Good afternoon, Mr. Campbell."

"Mr. Campbell?" he said, obviously amused. "My, aren't we formal today. How did your morning and afternoon go?"

"Not bad. I just got off the phone with Billy Hutchins. I asked him to work for me this season."

"That's great. The kid could use the money. Did one of the Atkins brothers show up at three?"

"Yes, he got here a few minutes ago. His brother will be here at eleven."

"Good. How about Maggie? Does she have enough food?"

Rachel felt that little bit of hope dwindle. If he was lining up protectors and checking on his dog, she wouldn't be seeing him today. "Maggie's fine. She's been following me around most of the day. I think she misses you, but she's tolerating me."

She heard him take in a long, slow breath, then let

it out. "Look," he said, "I probably won't see you until tomorrow night. I'm tied up today and I have that—"

"—meeting tomorrow. I know." There was nothing wrong with her intuition. She hadn't misunderstood his distance last night. "That's okay. Roy's here. He's all I need."

For a long moment, there was nothing but empty space on the line. Then he spoke quietly. "Well, I just wanted to wish you an early happy birthday, and make sure someone was there with you."

"Don't worry," she said, dredging up a cheerful tone to hide her hurt. "I'm in very good hands. Have a good rest of the day."

Again, it took him a while to reply. "You, too."

Rachel dropped the handset into the cradle, tears welling in her eyes. Whatever connection they'd had was over. And how pathetic she was, getting all excited because he'd shared something as incidental as her birthday with Billy Hutchins.

Grabbing a soda from the fridge, she walked briskly back to the game room, then picked up the remote and flopped down on the sofa to watch TV. Maggie jumped up on the sofa beside her, and Rachel saw her through watery eyes.

"Know what?" she said to the dog. "That guy you live with needs a great big kick in the pants. I don't know from one day to the next if he cares about me, or if he's hovering because of his sister, or if I'm just his something-to-do project."

Maggie snuggled close, and Rachel stroked her silky fur. "Know what else?" she whispered over the lump in her throat. "I think I'm in love with him."

* * *

Wednesday brought another day of rain and a jittery case of nerves Rachel could add to her missing-Jake doldrums. She practically haunted the weather channel, checking for updates. With the first official camping weekend of summer only two days away, the last thing she wanted to see was more precipitation—but that's what the weather gurus were forecasting. The pool was crystal clear and covered, and everything that had needed to be stained or painted was ready for her guests. She'd planned to have her summer help cut all the grass tomorrow. Unfortunately, it looked like that plan would have to be scratched. The lawns were bound to be sopping wet.

It rained when Roy Atkins showed up for work at 3:00 p.m. and added a tarp to the golf cart's canopy.

It rained for her meeting with her summer help at three-forty-five.

It was still raining at five-fifteen when displaced Brit, Max Stafford, called to say her new brochures were printed and ready for pickup. By then, she was so worked up, thinking about the birthday dinner she'd have to sit through, that she was more than eager to be on the road. That lump rose in her throat again. Because deep inside, she feared this dinner was simply an obligation—feared *she* was an obligation. But he'd made a promise and he would see it through regardless of how uncomfortable he made them both.

"Happy birthday to me," she whispered.

Jenna, Margo and her parents had called earlier in the day with birthday wishes, and when her dad left the room, her mom had asked nervously how the investigation was going. Hiding her own edginess, she replied that nothing had changed since she'd talked with her yesterday and the day before. Things were still good, and she believed they would stay that way. Now that the bones had been uncovered, there was no reason for any further trouble. If he was smart, her tormentor was long gone.

She glanced at the clock in the galley. Max had said he'd be open until six, and because Jake had mentioned having dinner at seven or later, she had time for a trip to town. She'd go. She'd leave a message on Jake's machine if he wasn't in, and she'd pick up her brochures—maybe drop a few off at the library.

Quickly striding into the game room, she dressed in jeans and a burgundy knit top, then donned the cross Jake had given her and went into the restroom to take a brush through her hair. She checked her reflection in the mirror. The lovely cross sparkled above her scalloped neckline, bringing back the bittersweet moment when he'd fastened it around her neck, then suddenly withdrawn. Sighing, Rachel stroked the cross—

—then stared numbly at the gold band beside it, catching the light.

She'd become so accustomed to its weight that she barely gave it a thought anymore. Or was she lying to herself? A lovely verse from Ecclesiastes rose with tender clarity in her mind and Rachel whispered the words. "To everything there is a season. A time to weep; a time to laugh. A time to mourn...and a time to dance."

This was her time, she suddenly realized. And she might have missed her chance to dance by holding on to the past too long.

Tears filled her eyes as she finally saw what Jake had to have seen: her manic need to clear David's name… her endless praise about his goodness…the ring on her finger that said she still belonged to him. If Jake had ever considered a loving relationship with her—and for a few days, she'd thought he might… Well, how much of that could any man take before he walked away?

Turning off the light, she went to her lunch counter and sank to a stool, memories flooding her mind. They were nice memories, but David was her past. With help from above, Jake could be her future. *If* he loved her, and if it wasn't already too late. "Please, God. Don't let it be too late," she whispered. Then she slipped the ring from her finger, laid it on the counter and went to the phone to leave Jake a message.

He answered on the second ring, sounding slightly breathless. Rachel cleared the tears from her throat. Already, this wasn't going well. She'd called at a bad time. "Hi. I didn't expect you to answer. I was just going to leave you a message."

"I just got in this minute. What's the message?"

"I wanted you to know that I have a few errands to run, but I'll be back in time for dinner. If it's still on."

"It's on," he returned.

At least he hadn't added that when he made a promise, he kept it.

"Is seven-thirty okay?" he asked.

"Seven-thirty's fine," she replied, hurting and wishing there'd been more warmth in his voice. "I'll see you before then."

Suddenly, he spoke tensely. "Did you say you're running errands? Tonight?"

"Yes. My new brochures are ready. I'm going to pick

them up, then drop a few at the library. I'll be back in plenty of time."

"Why are you doing this tonight?" he said impatiently. "The rain's really coming down out there, and the roads—"

Frustration overtook her sadness. "I'm doing it because I'm sick of feeling like a prisoner in my own—*store*. I'm through postponing my life, Jake. I'll see you soon."

"Rachel—"

"I'll see you soon," she repeated. Then she hung up, pulled on a clear hooded rain poncho from her stock, grabbed her purse and dashed across the driveway to her Explorer.

The winding roads coming up out of the valley were slick, and amid thick, dark storm clouds, thunder rumbled. Wind-whipped leaves flew by her windshield, her wipers doing double time. She would never admit it to Jake, but she was relieved when the rain-haloed, old-fashioned streetlights lining Charity's Main Street came into view.

The town was busy for a Wednesday evening, nearly all the parking spaces near the diner and hardware store filled. Hungry patrons clutching umbrellas hurried along the walks, heading for the diner's bright lights and blue plate specials. Rachel turned off Main Street onto Sassafras, then slowed when she reached Woodland Park where a wreath still hung on the black iron gate in memory of Leanne Hudson who'd died last year at the hands of a deeply disturbed man.

She parked in the street outside the huge, dramatically painted teal, cream and pink Victorian home that housed Stafford on Avon Printing. The words at the bottom of the sign in the front yard read Snooty Brit on site. Be courteous.

Thankful that the rain had eased a little, she sprinted across the sidewalk and up the steps to the porch. Max opened the door as she was reaching for the knob.

"You made good time in this nonsense," he said, gesturing her inside his artfully decorated entry. "How were the roads?"

"A little tricky, but I was climbing hills most of the way, so I wasn't driving through standing water."

She shed the transparent plastic hood on her poncho and smiled at the tall, white-haired man with the patrician good looks and elegant bearing. His dark pants were knife-creased, and a blue paisley ascot filled the collar of his pearl-gray silk shirt.

"Got something for me, Max?"

"Indeed, I do." He stepped to the gleaming mahogany sideboard that graced his wide foyer and took a box from the cabinet. There was a sample taped to the box. "Take a look now, and make sure it's to your liking."

Rachel smiled. Max was perfection in everything he did, but she scanned his work anyway. "Beautiful, Max. Thank you." She handed him a check from her shoulder bag, then clasped his hand. "Great to see you again."

"You can't stay for a moment?"

She shook her head. "I wish I could, but I'm on the clock and I have another stop to make. Come and see me at the campground sometime." Pulling up her hood again, she sent him a teasing smile. "I have Earl Grey and English breakfast tea."

"I shall do that," he said, chuckling as they said their goodbyes. "But in truth, I prefer coffee."

The library across the street was busy, too, although

she couldn't imagine why until she entered and saw three roll-away bookcases and a huge sign in the lobby that said BOOK SALE: Hardcovers $1.00, Paperbacks 25 cents. More Inside.

Rachel glanced at her watch, decided she had time to browse for a few titles for the game room, then joined the others going through the books. She couldn't quite bring herself to buy the romances she'd always loved with her own love life a shambles. But thanks to Emma Lucille Bridger's eagle eye, she scooped up four hardcover mysteries by an author she'd always enjoyed, and a few hidden picture books for the kids. Then with a wave to Emma Lu, she entered the library proper, added a dozen brochures to the Local Happenings rack, and carried her purchases to the desk to pay for them. She was back in the lobby and on her way to the door when Jillian Donner came inside, laughing and shaking the rain from her umbrella.

She pulled off her khaki rain hat. "Rachel, hi!"

"Hi, Jillian," she replied, then slipped into small talk. "Enjoying the weather?"

"No, it's awful," she said, still laughing. "But we need the rain, so we're trying not to complain. Right?" She half-turned, rolled her eyes, then spoke to Rachel. "Okay, I wasn't talking to myself. Nate was right behind me. I'm working the sale until nine, so Mr. Worrywart followed me to town to make sure I made it in one piece." The door opened. "Oh, here he is now. I was just telling Rachel—"

Rachel's hearing shut down, and the breath left her body as Nate Carter smiled and peeled back the hood on his navy windbreaker. The navy windbreaker with the seven-ten split emblem on the front—and a matching, much larger "rabbit's head" on the back. Her heart pounded like a trip hammer. *Please, God, don't let it be Nate.* But she was so afraid that it might be. Pieces of the puzzle she should have seen earlier began to fall into place. She needed to talk to Perris!

Be careful, she thought. After accusing Joe Reston, you need to be sure. Perris will eat you alive if you're wrong again.

No, she couldn't go to the chief. She had to talk to Jake.

Nate stepped closer, looked her over. "Are you okay, Rachel? You look…pale."

Focus! Don't let him see your fear! Forcing a laugh, she pinched some color into her cheeks. "I'm fine—just distracted. I'm still trying to get all my ducks in a row for my campground opening the day after tomorrow."

"Well, I hope it dries up out there before your guests come in. I've camped in the rain before and I don't recall liking it much." He ushered Jillian toward the library's inside door. "See you at the Memorial Day service at Woodland Park?"

She forced another smile as she exited, her plastic bag of books slung over her arm. "Yep. See you there."

"Careful on your way home."

"You, too," she called back.

Rachel raced across the street, dodged an oncoming car, then opened the door, tossed her purse and books on the passenger's seat of her Explorer and climbed behind the wheel. Her heart continued to pound. She had to get to Jake. She needed to discuss this logically, without her fears and snapping nerve endings getting in the way of clear thought. Jake had a cool head. *Jake.*

She started the car, waited for traffic to clear, then turned on her lights, backed into Max's driveway and reversed her direction. The pretty black antique light poles she'd noted on her way into town barely registered as she passed the diner, then the bakery, her tires shooting out plumes of rain water. Ben Caruthers was just leaving his hardware store as she approached, and he waved from beneath his umbrella. She beeped and slowed to avoid splashing him. Then she drove up the hill, passed Jenna's B & B, and accelerated onto the state route.

Sunset—if the sun were visible—was still two hours away, but the rain and rolling storm clouds had plunged Charity into a preternatural darkness that made her feel even more alone than she was. She swallowed, checked her rearview mirror and prayed.

"Please, God, don't let it be Nate. Please." The Explorer hit a pothole, then splashed over the rain-slick road again. How *could* it be Nate when he'd worked so hard with the other firefighters to save her business after her home was gone? Would he have set the fire, then risked his life in the smoke and flames to put it out? Somehow, she just couldn't wrap her mind around that. He was a decent man. They didn't come any better.

She was descending Crocker Hill with her wipers going full-force when blindingly bright headlights speared her rearview mirror and a vehicle shot up behind her. She tapped her brake to make him back off. Idiot kids just loved to race down this hill—sheer lunacy considering the lack of guardrails and the steep descent. Especially with the rain coming down so hard. She tapped her brake again.

The SUV sped forward—rammed her rear bumper.

Nerves jolting, Rachel gripped the wheel in a stranglehold and accelerated. This was no teenager playing hot wheels! She made a mad grab for her purse, fishtailed on the asphalt—grabbed for it again. She had to call 9-1-1 before she lost cell service! She shook the phone out of the side pocket, felt around and snatched it from the seat.

The SUV rammed her again, and Rachel cried out as the impact jarred the phone from her hand and it fell to the floor. "Sweet Jesus, help me!" she cried, and hit the gas pedal again. She was nearly to the bottom of the hill when the SUV stopped fooling around. Roaring into the left lane, it slammed into the Explorer's side and with another cry that dissolved into a thunderous crash of glass, snapped saplings and scraped hemlocks, Rachel plunged down through the dark, dense ground cover. Just before the air bag deployed and she crashed into a thick wall of mountain laurels, she turned her head and raised her right arm to shield her face. It exploded from the steering wheel with a massive crack, thrusting her back against the seat.

Then all was quiet except for the patter of rain on the Explorer's roof and cracked windshield.

She was only half conscious of the smell and powdery grit from the air bag, only half conscious of the pain in her right cheekbone and a numb sensation in her right arm. Her head swam, throbbed, and her chest and ribs ached in a way she'd never felt before. But she knew she was alive because "dead" couldn't hurt this badly.

"Thank you, Jesus," she whispered again and again. "Thank you." She sat there for another moment before she attempted to get her bearings. Her car hadn't merely hit the laurels; it seemed to have scaled them, putting the car in a slight upward slant with its one functioning headlamp lighting the hemlocks in front of her.

She stirred slowly, tried to move a little at a time. And she tasted blood. That's when she heard someone huffing and puffing through the snapping underbrush. For an instant her heart leaped with hope, then in a nervous rush of adrenaline, she realized that he could be the person who'd run her off the road. Rachel shut her eyes, slumped over toward the passenger's seat—went still as death. She held her breath. *Please, God. Let him be a friend.*

Heavy breathing and guttural panting carried to her, along with the sound of laurel branches scraping her door as it was pulled open. Light flared behind her closed eyelids as someone shone a flashlight over the side of her face.

But when no one tried to rouse her or ask if she was all right, she knew the man standing over her wasn't there to help. He stood there for a time, while Rachel's lungs begged for air and threatened to reveal her. Then he reached inside, clicked off her one working headlight, closed her door and left. But not before he murmured, "I'm sorry, Rachel."

Tears formed behind her closed eyelids. She knew that voice.

It seemed like forever until the vehicle on the road above her roared away and Rachel knew it was safe to move. Drawing another acrid breath, she clicked her headlight back on and took stock of her injuries. She moved her legs…moved her right arm again and realized it might be broken. Still, she slid from under the deflated air bag and with a hard shove, opened the car door. Her head spun a little as she got out on wobbly legs and, using the car for support, moved cautiously through the cold drizzle and matted laurel branches. Then her head spun a lot. She moved faster across the forest floor toward the steep bank, terrified she wouldn't make it to the road before she lost consciousness. Then everything began to go black, the wet ground rushed up to claim her, and she knew her fears were well founded.

Jake glanced at the clock again, and his earlier annoyance turned to uneasiness. Seven-forty-seven. She should have been here by now. Even if she was ticked off at him, she would have been on time or let him know she'd be late. He crossed to the kitchen phone to call her cell again—and again, it went directly to voice mail. Then snatching the phone book from a hook on the wall, he looked up printers. There was only one listed: Stafford on Avon. A half minute later, a cultured Englishman's recorded voice told him that office hours were from nine to six daily, but if he absolutely, positively had to be reached, Jake could call the following number. Three phone calls later, his nerves were corkscrews. She'd left the printer's place around six, and the library twenty minutes later.

With a quick "Stay here, Maggie," Jake grabbed his sidearm, rushed into the rain to his truck and gunned it out of the driveway—high beams on and wipers flashing. Charity was a five-mile, straight shot from the valley, so there was only one route she could have taken. If she'd started for home and didn't make it, he'd find her. His heart hammered against his ribcage and he tried to ignore the sick feeling in his stomach. There could be a lot of reasons why she hadn't shown. She could have had car trouble. Flat tires were rare, but they happened. Electrical failures happened, too. But deep in his gut, he knew she was in trouble of another kind and for the first time in decades, he murmured a shaky prayer that came straight from his soul. "Please, God, she's a good woman. Let her be okay because I—" He swallowed the emotion in his throat. "Because I won't be able to handle it if anything happens to her."

He loved her. It made no difference that he wasn't ready for it; he loved her. "Please," he whispered fervently, "I'll do anything You want me to do. Just keep her safe."

His tires ate up the highway. Although thunder rumbled overhead and lightning flashed in the distance, the rain was letting up a little, increasing visibility. He was midway up Crocker Hill when he saw a dim glow in the woods. His heart nearly leaped from his chest.

Pulling onto the right shoulder, he pushed on his hazard lights, grabbed a flashlight from the backseat and raced across the road. He heard her call out for help before he reached the edge.

"Rachel!" he shouted hoarsely.

"Yes! Yes, Jake, I'm here!"

He saw her in the beam of his flashlight, making her way up the steep incline—and his spirits plummeted. She looked like a horror show extra. Her wet hair was flattened to her head, her face was streaked with dirt and she seemed to be favoring her right arm. He half ran, half slid down the bank toward her. Saplings and brush scraped his arms and legs as his mind sent up repeated thanks to God. "Are you okay?"

"Yes! Yes, I'm all right."

He reached her, wrapped her in his arms—felt her

wet body quake from the cold. "Oh, Rachel, thank God."

"Yes, thank God," she repeated on a soft breath.

A thousand questions ran through his mind, but his first priority was to get her to safety. She was a good driver. It was no accident that her Explorer ended up in a ravine. "Come on. Let's get you to my truck. Do you hurt anywhere? Can you make it up the hill?"

"Yes, my arm hurts, but it's okay. Jake, it was Nate Carter. I know his voice. Nate did this. And I think I know why."

The rage he felt knowing that a friend had done this to her nearly cancelled his joy at finding her. But now wasn't the time to go off like a Roman candle. "I'll call Perris from the truck. We need to get you to the hospital."

"No! If you tell Perris that I said it was Nate, he'll drag his feet."

"Rachel—"

"In the meantime, Nate could get away. He's going to run. His house is only ten minutes from here. If you hurry, we can get to his place before Perris does."

"No. We're going to the ER."

She didn't say another word until they were under way with the heater in his truck going full-force. What she said gave him an instant headache.

"Take me to Nate's."

"Rachel, you're hurt and you're running on pure adrenaline. When it wears off—"

"Jake, I need to see him! And I need for him to see me! Obviously, he believes I'm dead or he would have finished what he started. I want him to know *right now* that he didn't win!"

He released an impatient breath, clicked on his high beams—slowed his wipers. She was cold, wet and leaning into the warm air flowing from the vents, but she seemed relatively clearheaded. Maybe she did need a face-to-face with Nate. "Okay, we'll drive to Carter's, but we're waiting there for Perris. I'll radio him as soon as we get to the top of the hill. Now tell me exactly what happened."

Eight minutes later, they slowed to a stop on the right side of the road opposite Nate Carter's long driveway. Jake backed up a little, giving them a clear view of the white house and garage fifty or sixty yards away, and the thin woods behind them. Tall pines lined the right side of the driveway, their branches trimmed halfway up the trunks.

The entire area was as dark and still as a tomb, and Rachel released a frustrated groan. "We missed him. He's gone."

"If he came back here at all. But there's a BOLO out on him, so there's a good chance he'll be picked up."

Jake reached for his radio. "I'll call Perris and see if he's still on his way. If not, we're out of here and headed to the ER to have you checked out." As she'd recounted the crash on their way here, she'd told him she'd lost consciousness for a while and had come to just minutes before he arrived. She probably had a concussion in addition to whatever was wrong with her arm.

Rachel's voice rose. "Jake, look! A light went on in the garage!"

He put the walkie down and unsnapped the holster on his hip. Before he could say a word, the garage door opened and a dark SUV rolled out. It paused for a long moment, its headlights finding them. Then suddenly it rushed straight for them.

"He sees us! Rachel, get out of the truck!"

"Jake!"

"Now!"

Everything happened in split seconds. Rachel leaped from the truck, and Jake hit the gas—shot across the road to block the driveway's entrance. The SUV barreled forward at top speed—aimed for the narrow space between the first skinned pine tree and the front of Jake's truck.

Jake dove to the passenger's side—braced for impact.

The SUV slammed the front of the truck—spun it clockwise toward the road. Then it struck the tree in a sickening crunch of metal and shattered glass.

It took Jake a moment to register that it was all over. Then he climbed out of the cab to see Rachel running toward him. She threw her arms around him. "Are you all right? Tell me you're okay!"

"Yeah," he said shakily, holding her close. "Yeah, I'm all right." His heart was racing and his pulse wasn't far behind, but if he was hurt, he didn't know it yet. He turned toward Nate's mangled SUV—saw him slumped over the steering wheel.

Then he set Rachel back from him, pulled his cell phone from his belt and handed it to her. "Call 9-1-1. I'll check on Nate." But he feared it was already too late for an ambulance.

As they awaited treatment in the ER, Perris had taken their statements and threatened action for their interference, then finally agreed that Nate had chosen his fate.

He then told them in confidence that one way or the other, Nate hadn't planned on coming back—as evidenced by the note he left.

Addressed to Jillian and left on his kitchen table, it was a sad reminder of the note he'd left on her table five years ago. It contained his heartfelt regret that they'd never have a life together—his dream since he'd fallen for her in high school. There was also a confession. One night, after seeing the evidence of another of Donner's beatings, Nate confronted Bryce and demanded that the abuse be stopped. When Bryce laughed at the gun in his hand, Nate had snapped. Knowing that Jillian would inherit the land, he'd buried Donner on the Trehern property. But then Rachel acquired the land, arranged to have it developed…and once again, Nate did what he had to do to ensure his future with Jillian.

Rachel had absorbed the information with mixed emotions. The tone of the note was remorseful, but there was no justification for what he'd done.

Later, in the ER as they waited for the doctor to discharge them, Jake pulled the curtains closed around the narrow bed where Rachel sat, and sank to the gurney beside her. X-rays had shown a hairline fracture of her braced right arm, but aside from the muscle aches and bruising that was already starting, she was fine.

"So, David's off the hook now."

"Yes," she replied. "I still don't understand why Perris kept pushing for his guilt. Maybe he just doesn't like me, or maybe he resented my interference and never really believed that David did it. But yes, it's over." She dropped her voice and looked at him. "It's all in the past now. All of it."

Jake took her left hand in his—stroked his thumb over her empty ring finger.

"It was time," she murmured, her eyes so full of love that he couldn't have mistaken it for anything else. And once again, Jake thanked God—for their lives, and for the promise of love that hung between them like a heart-swelling song at the end of a Disney movie. It was corny and sentimental, but he wanted the song to last forever.

He spoke softly. "You know I'm in love with you, don't you?"

Tears sparkled in her green eyes and she nodded. "Do you know I love you, too?"

"I do now." Smiling again, he raised her hand and kissed her fingertips. "Do you also know that I didn't want to love you? I fought it tooth and nail from day one, and for a while, I was winning the battle. But apparently God saw things differently."

"And because He knows what's best for us—" Rachel whispered, turning into him and meeting his dark eyes.

"—we should never disappoint Him," Jake whispered back, then covered her mouth with his own.

EPILOGUE

Six months later. November.

Rachel smiled as she heard the door open, and Jake came inside the pretty log home that was hers now, too. He'd been gone all day, helping Reverend Landers and a few other men from St. John's paint and lay new floor tile in the church's community room. This year, St. John's was hosting the Thanksgiving Day dinner for elderly residents and those who couldn't be with their families. Maggie was outside, terrorizing the local squirrel population.

Quickly smoothing a wrinkle on the tablecloth, she lit the candles on either side of her pretty fall flower arrangement and went into the living room. He was just slipping off his boots.

"Hey," he said, smiling and giving her turquoise, berry and white sweater an appreciative once-over. "You look pretty for a Wednesday."

She laughed. "Do I usually look like a hag?"

Chuckling, he walked over to her to take her in his arms. "No, you look beautiful every day of the week. You just look exceptionally beautiful today." He kissed her softly. "Do I smell spaghetti sauce?"

"Lasagna. It occurred to me today that we haven't had it since—since we warmed it up when we got home that night." Despite everything, she still felt a little sad about Nate's death. Oddly, although that night had been terrifying, she now associated lasagna with happiness because that night things had finally fallen into place for her and Jake.

She found her smile again. "Anyway, I called your mom and asked for her recipe, which I imagined was the same as yours. I've decided that lasagna should be our 'celebration' food." She grinned. "Now that I think about it, we should have had it at our wedding reception."

He tipped his head curiously. "So what are we celebra—" He stopped abruptly and his smile stretched wide, lighting the brown eyes she loved. "You picked up the kit today?"

She nodded, nearly bursting with excitement. "If my calculations are correct, we're going to be very busy the first week in June."

Rachel shrieked as Jake scooped her up—spun her in a circle, and peppered happy kisses over her face. Then he slid her to the floor again, and they settled into a long, slow, deeply loving, forever kind of kiss. They were so blessed, Rachel thought as sighs broke between their lips and they smiled into each other's eyes. Six months ago, she'd thought she'd never have a child of her own, and Jake had longed for a family but was afraid to hope it would happen.

Now they were married, and there was a tiny little Campbell on the way.

"God's given us a good life," Jake murmured.

"Yes, He has," Rachel whispered, tipping her face up for another kiss. "And I have a feeling it's going to get even better."

* * * * *

Dear Reader,

Welcome back to Charity, Pennsylvania, where friendship, church and a strong sense of community keep the town a warm, interesting place in which to live—despite the recent capture of a serial killer and the skeleton that was just found on Rachel Patterson's property.

If you've read this book—or anything else I've written—you probably picked up on my love of small towns and woodsy settings. It's where I live, where I met and married my soul mate and where we raised our family. It's where "nature walks" along our country road with our grandkids offer up fascinating things like snails and salamanders in mud banks, and crayfish in the super-skinny creek nearby. It's where we search the milkweeds for monarch butterfly caterpillars, and check out the neighbor's shaggy Scotch Highland cattle. And—sometimes—it's where I see and feel God's presence even more acutely than I do in church.

Wishing you Peace, Joy and Happy Reading,

Lauren Nichols

Questions for Discussion

1. Feelings of guilt and disloyalty plague Rachel when she finds herself being attracted to Jake. Do you believe there's an appropriate time to mourn a beloved spouse before moving on? Or do you believe that love is a gift from God and should be joyfully accepted whenever it's given?

2. Jake's sister's violent death caused him to blame God—to completely move away from Him. Eventually, his anger faded, but by that time life had become busy and his faith had been back-burnered so long that he didn't miss it. Was there a time when life was so consuming that you did the same? If you returned to God, what did it take to bring you back?

3. Do you believe that people who don't attend church, yet believe in God, can be saved? What about people who don't believe? Will God reward them if they've lived good lives?

4. Did you feel any sympathy for the villain who killed to protect someone he loved?

5. What are your feelings about people who do bad things for what they believe to be "good" reasons? Short of murder, can these actions ever be justified?

6. Rachel finds comfort in the scriptures, particularly the psalms and those mentioned in this book.

Are there favorite passages in the Bible that speak to you?

7. It was difficult for Jake and Rachel to admit their love for each other—even to themselves—because of a betrayal in his past, and Rachel's loyalty to the husband she'd lost. Was there a time when you wanted to tell someone that you cared, yet held back because admitting your feelings would make you uncomfortable, or you feared your feelings wouldn't be reciprocated? Did you regret it?

8. Small towns like Charity have their share of gossips. How do you feel about gossip in general? Do you always believe what you hear? Does it end with you or do you pass it on?

9. Before sharing information that could hurt someone—even if the information is true—do you ever consider the Golden Rule—"Do unto others as you would have them do unto you"?

10. Rachel is overheard accusing Joe Reston of murder, and is swiftly and soundly taken to task for it. Have you ever wished you could take back something you've said or done?

11. The chief of police in this story is an arrogant man who does his job, but his social skills leave much to be desired. How do you deal with people who are cold and insulting for no apparent reason? Do you turn the other cheek? Or do you try to under-

stand what made them that way and include them in your prayers?

12. *On Deadly Ground* opens in the spring of the year when the woods are greening, and all around there's a feeling of rebirth. Dandelions fill the fields, songbirds seem to come out of hiding and fawns and newborn elk calves make their wide-eyed appearance in this lovely world God has created for us. Do you ever see and feel God's presence in natural settings?

INSPIRATIONAL

Inspirational romances to warm your heart & soul.

TITLES AVAILABLE NEXT MONTH

Available September 13, 2011

LONE DEFENDER
Heroes for Hire
Shirlee McCoy

HIDDEN IN THE EVERGLADES
Guardians, Inc.
Margaret Daley

THE LAST TARGET
Christy Barritt

DEEP COVER
Undercover Cops
Sandra Orchard

LISCNM0811

Love Inspired®

Everything Montana Brown *thought* she knew about love and marriage goes awry when her parents split up. Shaken, she heads to Mule Hollow, Texas, to take a chance on an old dream—being a cowgirl…while trying to resist the charms of a too-handsome cowboy. A wife isn't on rancher Luke Holden's wish list. But the Mule Hollow matchmakers are fixin' to lasso Luke and Montana together—with a little faith and love.

Her Rodeo Cowboy

by Debra Clopton

Available September wherever books are sold.

www.LoveInspiredBooks.com

LI87691